D1707165

THE CHESTER KILLINGS

A SNOWDONIA MURDER MYSTERY

A DI Ruth Hunter Crime Thriller #18

SIMON MCCLEAVE

STAMFORD

THE CHESTER KILLINGS

By Simon McCleave

A DI Ruth Hunter Crime Thriller
Book 18

First published by Stamford Publishing Ltd in 2024

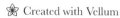 Created with Vellum

BOOKS BY SIMON McCLEAVE

THE DI RUTH HUNTER SERIES

THE DC RUTH HUNTER MURDER CASE SERIES

THE ANGLESEY SERIES - DI LAURA HART

'We also know that when a woman stands up and speaks truth to power that there will be attempts to put her down, and so I'm not going to be put down. I'm not going to go anywhere.'

Maxine Walters

'Come, you spirits that tend on mortal thoughts, unsex me here,
    And fill me from the crown to the toe top-full
    Of direst cruelty. Make thick my blood.
    Stop up th'access and passage to remorse,
    That no compunctious visitings of nature
    Shake my fell purpose .... Come, thick night,
    And pall thee in the dunnest smoke of hell,
    That my keen knife see not the wound it makes,
    Nor heaven peep through the blanket of the dark,
    To cry "Hold, hold!"'

LADY MACBETH

Your FREE book is waiting for you now!

Get your FREE copy of the prequel to
the DI Ruth Hunter Series NOW
http://www.simonmccleave.com/vip-email-club
and join my VIP Email Club

To Dad

David McCleave (1944-2023)

RIP x

Prologue

July 2021

IT WAS a mild summer's night as the young man staggered along the Shropshire Union Canal which snaked its way through the city of Chester. The air smelled of barbecued food and cigarette smoke. The thudding bass of dance music could be heard somewhere in the distance. He looked up and squinted at the night sky. He'd been out at after work drinks in the fashionable bars of central Chester, but he wasn't drunk. He'd only had a few pints. And he'd avoided grabbing any fast food on the way home, because during the summer he'd been training at the gym trying to hone his beach body and six-pack. Originally from North Wales, he had now settled across the border in Cheshire. Some of his more fervent Welsh mates said he was 'a bloody traitor'. He ignored them and laughed it off. In fact even though he knew it was snobby, he thought there was a better class of person over in Chester. More importantly, the women were much better looking too. At least that's what he told his mates back in Wales. He wasn't actually sure it was true. Maybe they just had more money.

Glancing behind, he saw there was a figure with a hoodie walking along the canal path about twenty yards behind him. He didn't think anything of it. He'd walked this path hundreds of times before as his apartment overlooked the waterway. And it was always relatively busy until the early hours, especially on a Friday and Saturday night.

He smiled to himself when he thought of the cute blonde girl he'd been chatting to in *Bar Lounge*. She had a cracking figure and, even though she was a bit thick, he'd love to get her into bed. He'd managed to persuade her to give him her number, so he'd drop her a few flirty texts when he got home. Then he'd get her into bed and that would be that. He'd *ghost* her. He had no desire to have a girlfriend. He was far too young. As his taid said, you just need to sow your wild oats while you're young. He got the feeling that his taid might have regretted getting married to his nain at only nineteen.

When he thought about his high-flying job in recruitment – 55k a year and a company car, thank you very much – his apartment and his lifestyle in general, he felt proud of how far he'd come. Born in a tiny two-bedroom house in the Wrexham suburb of Rhos, he'd had five brothers and sisters. The house had been a chaotic mess, mainly because his father was a drunk and spent most of his free time in the local pub. His mum was timid and didn't like to cause a fuss. He couldn't wait to get away to university in Manchester for three years. And now Chester.

Chester was a well-heeled cathedral city in Cheshire, England, close to the England/Wales border. It dated back to Roman times and still had remnants of the city walls and even a small amphitheatre from that time. The centre of the city was popular with tourists and shoppers, with its cobbled stone walkways and black and white medieval buildings – although many were restored in Victorian times.

For a moment, the young man felt compelled to peer up at the night sky again. There was something slightly different about it tonight. With no clouds to obscure them, the stars seemed unusually clear. The moon was full, low in the sky, and seemed to have a pinkish hue. He'd heard on the radio that it was a 'blood moon'. The radio presenter had joked that ancient cultures like the Incas thought the 'blood moon' symbolised impending doom, death, or the overthrowing of a king. The young man just thought it looked bigger than normal which was a bit freaky. As for its symbolic meaning to the Incas, that was just bollocks wasn't it?

Hearing a noise behind him, he glanced back and saw that the figure following him was now only ten yards behind.

Blimey, he's going like the clappers.

Before he could see their face, the figure had blown a huge cloud of vape which seemed to envelop them for a few seconds.

He remembered he had a couple of cold beers in the fridge for when he got home. *Nice one!* Then he'd either play on his PlayStation, watch the footie on the telly or some porn on his phone. It depended on whether or not his flatmate was in.

'Wayne?' called a voice.

He turned. It was the person behind him calling his name.

'Hello?' he answered with a frown as he stopped and squinted back at them. He didn't recognise the voice that had called out.

'Wayne Braddock?'

The figure approached and stopped.

Wayne peered at them. 'Yeah?'

CRACK!

Something smashed hard against the side of his head.

Everything seemed to go black for a moment.

He staggered.

A blinding eruption of pain.

Jesus Christ! he gasped.

He tried to get his breath as his head reverberated with an ear-splitting white noise.

What the ...?

He managed to regain his footing for a second.

Looking down, he saw that the figure was holding a hammer in one hand and a long screwdriver in the other.

Shit!

'You bastard!' they hissed through gritted teeth. Nostrils flared and a mouth twisted with utter fury.

'What the fuck ... are ... you doing?' he mumbled through the pain. He was terrified.

The screwdriver came towards him, but he managed to dodge out of the way.

Panic.

It came again and this time plunged into the flesh of his bicep.

'Argh!' he cried in agony.

He turned and tried to sprint down the canal path, fearing for his life.

Please God, don't let them kill me. Please.

He held his arm and winced at the searing white hot pain he felt. His legs were heavy and unsteady. He didn't understand.

I'm going to lose my balance.

A sickening fear that throttled him.

Run. Just run! Don't fall over.

Grunting, panting, muttering under his breath as he stumbled.

Then a piercing pain in the middle of his back. He'd been stabbed with the screwdriver again.

Losing his balance, he fell face first onto the pathway.

CRACK!

The figure kicked him hard in the head.

A sickening, blinding wave of pain and stupefying confusion.

He gasped.

He grabbed at a wrist and kicked out blindly.

'No, no, no,' he wheezed, shaking his head desperately as he fought for his life.

A scream that was trapped inside by utter panic.

A dark, crushing acceptance.

It was over.

This was it.

He had nothing. No fight left.

Silence.

A gloved hand moved towards his throat.

Then the bloody screwdriver came into view.

Glancing up at the clear sky, he saw the patterns of stars so many millions of miles away. And above that the blood moon.

It was the last thing he saw before the final darkness came.

Chapter 1

It was morning, and Detective Inspector Ruth Hunter of the North Wales Police was standing in front of the CID team at Llancastell Police Station. It had been over three months since Ruth had been shot and nearly killed during a police operation. She'd had a cardiac arrest and flatlined, and doctors told her she was lucky to be alive. In the first few weeks of her recovery, her overwhelming feeling had been that now she was in her early 50s it was time to call it a day. She'd been a police officer since her early 20s and had accumulated a more than healthy pension. She and her partner Sarah were in the process of trying to adopt an eleven-year-old boy, Daniel, whom they currently had temporary foster care for. They wanted him to be a permanent part of their family. Being a police officer was dangerous and exhausting, and Ruth had given over thirty years of her life to the service.

However, as the weeks of recovery went on she began to reassess her retirement plans. The days dragged. Daniel was at school and Sarah spent much of her time caring for her sick mother, Doreen. Ruth realised that without the cut and thrust of police work her life was incredibly boring. While she was still able to work as a detective, she knew that's where her heart belonged.

When she'd arrived at Llancastell CID that morning, she was aware that many in the CID team expected her to announce her retirement. She had been incredibly touched that so many of them were desperate for her to stay. In the six years since her move to the North Wales Police force from the London Met, she and the Llancastell CID team had been through a lot. They had lost colleagues along the way. And Ruth had lost her partner Sian in a police operation at Solace Farm.

So it was incredibly humbling when there seemed to be a collective sigh of relief as she announced to them that she intended to stay.

She could see the look of joy on Detective Sergeant Nick Evan's face in particular. After a rocky start, she and Nick had a very strong working relationship that had also developed into a deep friendship. Ruth was even godmother to Nick's daughter Megan.

Having told the CID team of her decision, Ruth watched as everyone began to move back to their desks to start the day's work. She was looking forward to a couple of days of routine paperwork and a few low-level crimes.

But then she noticed that Detective Constable Jim Garrow had just put down the phone. He looked over at her with a baffled expression.

'Everything all right, Jim?' she asked, sensing his unease.

'Not really, boss,' he replied.

'What's up?'

'Uniformed officers have found a body in Chester.'

Ruth frowned. 'Chester's in England.'

'Only some of it, boss. Apparently the victim was

found on the border, so half the body is lying in England and the other half in North Wales,' Garrow said, looking puzzled.

'What? That's a new one,' she said thoughtfully. Then she turned to Nick and threw him her car keys.

'Where are we going?' he asked uncertainly.

'I can't sit here chatting all day,' she replied with a knowing smile. 'We've got a murder to solve. You drive, I'll smoke.'

'I thought you quit?'

'Come on,' Ruth groaned as she headed for the double doors.

Chapter 2

Ruth and Nick raced up the A483 passing the turning to Wrexham as they headed towards Chester.

'Just like old times,' Nick remarked as they sped along.

'It's been a while,' Ruth admitted as she looked out to her left and watched the countryside fly by.

Nick reached over to the stereo and turned up the music. *Gimme Shelter* by *The Rolling Stones* was playing.

'This okay?' he asked, referring to the music.

Ruth gave him a curious smile. 'What are you asking me for?' she joked. 'You normally play what you want and make some disparaging remarks about my musical taste.'

Nick's eyes widened with mock offence. 'I don't do that ...'

Ruth raised an eyebrow. 'You once told me that *Duran Duran* were a band who wished they were *Roxy Music* but didn't have the talent so made up for that with ridiculous pretentiousness.'

'Did I? Well it's completely true. Plus, they're the band who wrote the lyric *you're about as easy as a nuclear war.*'

'Okay, okay,' Ruth conceded. 'I was about fifteen when

I liked the New Romantic bands.' She gestured to the car stereo. 'Who's this then?'

Nick frowned as if that was a ridiculous question. 'Erm ... *The Rolling Stones.*'

'Oh right. I quite like this one. My dad hated *The Rolling Stones*. He said they were 'druggies.' He preferred *The Beatles.*'

Nick chortled. 'Of course. *The Beatles* - a band famous for never taking any drugs but wrote their last three albums high on marijuana and LSD!'

'Oh yeah.' Ruth rolled her eyes as they left the A483 and headed for the centre of Chester. 'I never thought about it like that.'

'I'm pretty sure you're going to be hard pushed to find any band who hasn't taken drugs,' Nick stated.

'Except *Sir Cliff Richard*,' Ruth said dryly.

'He's not human. He's a genderless Christian cyborg,' Nick joked.

'Is he?' Ruth smiled. 'Good to know.'

They turned left down Sealand Road close to the River Dee. There were houses to their right and a leafy park called The Cop to the left. It had once been the site of the Cheshire Cheese Warehouse, exporting 7,000 tons of cheese a year to London in the 18th century. Now it was a lovely park with a children's playground and 'a graffiti wall.' At the far side was a raised bank known as the Bund which was a defence against the River Dee flooding the area.

Ruth looked out at the park and saw a little group of mothers pushing buggies and pushchairs as they headed for the nearby playground. It seemed so long since she'd pushed her daughter Ella across Clapham Common to the swings over towards Abbeville village. And then she thought of her ex-husband Dan, Ella's father, who had had an affair and moved to Australia where he had started a new life and a new family.

Jesus, that's nearly twenty-five years ago, she realised to her horror.

The sunshine came through the high oak and silver birch trees that lined the park's perimeter. It cast dappled shadows on the pavement and road.

Ruth wound down the window and let the fresh air blow in her face for a few seconds. It felt warm and sweet.

Then she pulled out a packet of cigarettes, took one and lit it. She took a deep drag and then blew a plume of smoke out of the window and watched as the wind snatched it away.

'You know half of that ends up back in the car and inside my lungs,' Nick said, half joking.

Ruth rolled her eyes. 'Shut up and drive.'

A few minutes later, Nick pulled the car left and they saw the Shropshire Union Canal snaking away to their right.

'The Shroppie,' he said, as he gestured to the narrow waterway.

'The what?' Ruth asked.

'That's what they call the Shropshire Union Canal. You can get all the way from here to Liverpool and Manchester. Built by Thomas Telford.'

Ruth shook her head. 'Yeah, okay. Thanks for the history lesson. I do know who Thomas Telford is.' She was lying. She had no idea who he was, although she had heard his name before.

Nick raised an eyebrow dubiously. 'Okay. Who is Thomas Telford then?' he asked, calling her out.

Ruth gave him an amused smile. 'Isn't he that red-headed bloke who was in that 80s band *Thompson Twins*?'

Nick laughed. 'Nice try,' he said sarcastically. 'He was a famous Scottish engineer. You know the place Telford?'

'Yes, of course,' Ruth said defensively.

'It's named after him. He built the Menai Bridge for starters.'

'Oh, right.' Ruth felt a little silly that she didn't know any of that. 'Come on, let's park up before you start talking again and I fall asleep.'

Nick gave her a look of mock offence. 'You're very rude.'

'I know, I've been told it's part of my charm,' she quipped.

The towpath was a hive of activity. Uniformed police cars had blocked off the access roads, and the towpath had been taped off by blue and white police evidence tape. There were about a dozen police officers in high-vis jackets redirecting traffic or explaining to people that they couldn't walk along the canal's towpath.

Ruth noticed that their jackets lacked the Welsh word *Heddlu* for Police.

'Here we go,' Nick said, as he parked close to a dark navy-coloured scene of crime forensics van.

As they got out, Ruth could feel the heat of the day as the blue sky above them was virtually cloudless. The Astra 2-litre's aircon had disguised how hot the day was already even though it was only mid-morning. The air was clammy.

Ruth took out her sunglasses and popped them on.

That's better, she thought. *Now I can stop squinting. I've got deep enough crow's feet as it is.*

She and Nick headed down a short grassy bank to the pathway and approached the young female uniformed officer who was manning the police cordon and carrying a clipboard.

They took out their warrant cards and showed them to her.

'DI Hunter and DS Evans, Llancastell CID,' Ruth explained.

The officer had long black hair pulled back tightly into a ponytail, and more than a decent amount of makeup. She also had bright red nail varnish.

I would have been told to go and scrub my face by my sarge if I'd turned up to work like that, Ruth thought to herself. However, she was pleased that female officers now wore the same uniforms as their male colleagues, and could wear their hair or makeup however they pleased. It was a far cry from the dark old days of the early 90s when she was called 'love', had to make senior officers cups of tea, and got the occasional slap on the backside.

The officer looked confused. 'Llancastell, ma'am?'

'This is a joint investigation between North Wales Police and Cheshire Police,' Ruth explained.

She nodded. 'Oh right.'

Nick looked at her. 'What have we got constable?'

'Victim is a young white male. Mid-20s,' she explained calmly. 'Looks like he was stabbed several times, sir.'

'Who's the officer in charge here?' Ruth asked.

'DI Simon Weaver,' she explained.

Ruth wasn't sure, but she thought she caught a hint from the constable that she wasn't a fan of DI Weaver.

'Thanks,' Nick said politely as they ducked under the police evidence tape and walked along the towpath.

Ruth saw a brightly decorated canal barge that was moored opposite. 'Constable, has anyone been over to speak to the people in that barge to see if they saw anything?'

'I don't think so, ma'am.'

'Can we do that as a matter of urgency?' Ruth asked

14

politely. 'I don't want them tootling off down the canal before anyone has spoken to them.'

'Will do, ma'am,' she replied.

As Nick and Ruth rounded the corner, they could see that a white forensic tent had been erected over the pathway, presumably where the body had been found. There were several scene of crime officers – SOCOs – in their white nitrile suits, masks and white rubber boots.

'You ever encountered DI Weaver before?' Ruth asked Nick under her breath.

He nodded. 'Used to play rugby against him years ago. He played for Chester first fifteen. Pretty decent fly half. Bit of a prick, but he liked a drink which made him a good bloke in my book back in the day.'

'How long ago was this?' Ruth asked as they approached the forensic tent.

'I was still in uniform … so quite a while.'

A figure dressed in a forensic suit approached them with a confident stride.

The man pulled down his mask. He had a blond-coloured beard and looked as if he was in his late 30s.

'DI Hunter?' he enquired.

Ruth nodded. It had to be DI Weaver.

'Nick,' Weaver said with a knowing smile. 'Been a while since we locked horns.' His face was sweaty from wearing the suit in the heat.

'You still play?' Nick asked.

'I tried the veterans for a while,' he said, 'but I kept getting injured. My DCI told me to quit.'

'Yeah, sounds familiar,' Nick said.

'So, half in Wales and half in England,' Ruth stated with a quizzical look. 'You think it's deliberate?'

Weaver shrugged. 'Not from the looks of it, but who knows?'

'Do we know anything about the victim yet?' Nick asked.

'Not really. No wallet, no phone. He was wearing expensive clothes and a designer watch. We've got a set of keys from his pocket but no way of identifying what they're for.'

'Any idea how long he's been here?' Ruth asked.

'I'm assuming he was attacked last night,' Weaver replied.

Ruth narrowed her eyes. 'Do you think he was mugged?'

Weaver took a few seconds to reply. 'That would have been the first assumption with the missing wallet and phone …'

'But?' Ruth asked, raising a quizzical eyebrow.

'It was a nasty, violent attack. Seven stab wounds from something like a screwdriver. Nasty wound to his temple too. Either the killer was off their head on something, or the attack was personal and deliberate.'

'And due to the jurisdiction, we have to run this as a joint investigation?' Ruth asked, although she knew the answer.

'That's what my super says.' Weaver didn't sound happy at the prospect, and he wasn't doing much to hide it. 'My suggestion is that we base ourselves at Chester Town Hall Police Station on Northgate Street. It's only two miles from here.'

Nick nodded in agreement. 'Makes sense.'

'Okay,' Ruth said warily. She was still trying to suss Weaver out to see what kind of copper he was. But being a couple of miles from the murder was probably a good idea.

Weaver looked at her. 'I know we're both DIs, but if we're based in Chester it seems sensible for me to lead as SIO on this?'

SIO stood for Senior Investigating Officer.

Hold your horses there mate, she thought, *we've just arrived*.

Ruth wasn't quite sure why Weaver had flagged up who was going to be in charge of the investigation already. It started to ring alarm bells. She needed to be clear from the outset that she wasn't going to be drawn into any kind of power play between the two forces.

Ruth locked eyes with him and responded firmly. 'I'll probably bring three or four detectives over from Llancastell. Let's just run two teams out of CID. We'll cover more ground. But if you'd like to run the morning briefings then I don't have any objection.' She was happy to concede that to him – but nothing else.

Weaver bristled a little and shrugged. 'Fair enough.' Maybe he thought Ruth was going to back down and let him run things.

'I guess we need to identify the victim as a priority,' Nick said.

'Let's see if we've had anyone reported missing this morning,' Weaver said. 'We can also run his prints and DNA through the databases but that's going to take a while.'

'And we might well draw a blank,' Ruth stated. The UK's national database of fingerprints and DNA, known as IDENT 1, only carried the profiles for those who had been charged or arrested for a criminal offence. However, even though it had been estimated that 10% of the UK population were on these databases, it still meant it was a long shot.

A female detective in a smart navy suit headed towards them from the direction where Ruth and Nick had parked. She was mixed race and her braided hair was pulled back off her face.

'DS Kennedy,' Weaver said to her as she approached.

'This is DI Hunter and DS Evans from North Wales Police. As I explained earlier, we're going to be running this as a joint investigation between our two forces.'

Kennedy gave them a half smile as she pulled out her notebook. 'Nice to meet you both.' Then she turned to Weaver. 'Think I've got something, boss. One of the uniformed officers thought she recognised the victim earlier.' She looked down at her notebook. 'A Wayne Braddock. I've done some checking and Braddock works at a recruitment consultants in the city centre. I gave them a call and he hasn't turned up for work this morning and hasn't called in sick. They seemed to think that was unusual.'

'Have you got an address?' Weaver asked.

'Yes.' She pointed back past the forensic tent. 'He lives in a first floor flat about half a mile further on down the canal front.'

'Maybe he was walking home when he was attacked,' Nick suggested.

Ruth raised an eyebrow. 'You said the uniformed officer thought she recognised the victim. Do you know how?'

Kennedy gave them a dark look. 'She worked on a rape case about a year ago. Wayne Braddock was arrested and charged with the offence. He was due to go to trial next month.'

'What happened?' Ruth asked, inferring that something had happened.

'The charges were dropped last week,' Kennedy explained.

'The victim and her family must have been devastated,' Ruth said, thinking out loud.

Ruth exchanged a look with Nick. She wondered if the dropping of charges was relevant to the attack.

Chapter 3

Ruth and Nick were now dressed in white nitrile forensic
suits and white rubber boots.

Nick came over as he secured his mask. 'You think the
dropping of the rape charge is significant?'

'What do you think?' Ruth asked.

'My instinct is that it's a very big coincidence.'

'Yeah, mine too.'

'And you know what Sherlock Holmes always said
about coincidences,' Nick said under his breath.

'Actually, I don't.'

He raised an eyebrow. 'The universe is rarely so lazy.'

'Ooh, I like that,' Ruth said, 'but I think we'll keep our
suspicions to ourselves for the time being.'

It wasn't that Ruth wanted to run the investigation
herself – although she would have been happier if she was.
It was that she suspected that if she or Nick flagged
anything up, Weaver was the sort of copper to take what
they'd found, investigate it with his own team and then
take credit if it led to anything. She'd met plenty of those

coppers in the Met, and she knew that sometimes it was prudent to play her cards close to her chest to start with.

Nick gave her a conspiratorial wink. 'I agree. Have more than you show, speak less than you know.'

Ruth rolled her eyes. 'Yeah, all right, Mr Rent A Quote.'

Weaver gave a gesture for them to follow him as they headed towards the forensic tent. As they arrived, a couple of SOCOs came out holding clear evidence bags.

Ruth took a step inside and saw the body of a young man lying on his back. His eyes were still open. His clothes were soaked in dark blood that had now congealed. His blue shirt had been ripped, possibly in a struggle with his attacker. As Weaver had described, she could see that he was well dressed and she spotted a silver TAG Heuer watch. From what she could remember, you wouldn't get much change out of £1,500 for that. She looked at his shoes. A pair of smart black Oxford brogues.

One SOCO was taking photographs of the body at the crime scene, while another held a small ruler to give the photographic records accurate measurements.

For a moment, Ruth was taken back to the first time she'd attended the scene of someone who had been attacked and murdered on the street. It had been the mid-90s and a drug dealer had been stabbed to death on an estate in Battersea, South London. Although it wasn't quite the bad old days of the 70s, forensics were still relatively basic. Fingerprints were still the gold standard of forensic evidence, although the use of DNA was becoming increasingly widespread. Colin Pitchfork had been the first man to be convicted of murder using DNA evidence back in 1988. However, the first national DNA database wasn't established until 1995. The main problem thirty years ago was that you needed a sizeable amount of blood, saliva, or semen to get an accurate DNA profile.

'Boss,' Nick said, breaking her train of thought. He was crouching down beside the victim and had used a pen to look under a ripped part of the shirt at the victim's chest.

'What is it?' she asked.

'Looks like the tattoo of a football club,' he explained, as he carefully lifted the material of the shirt. 'And it looks like he's from our neck of the woods.'

Weaver frowned. 'Why do you say that?'

Nick looked up at them both. 'Because this is a Wrexham FC tattoo.'

Chapter 4

Twenty minutes later, Ruth and Nick pulled up outside an apartment block that looked over the canal. While Weaver and Kennedy had gone to Braddock's place of work, Ruth and Nick were following up on the address they'd been given for Wayne Braddock.

The sun was blazing down as Ruth got out of the car. She was wearing her new sunglasses which felt unusually heavy on the bridge of her nose. They were Ray-Bans and had been a birthday present from Sarah. Ruth was used to wearing flimsy cheap sunglasses that she'd bought from a chemist or online.

A dark red narrowboat with an ornate floral pattern cruised past them along the water. A couple in their 70s were sitting at the back drinking coffee and taking in the views.

'I could definitely do with a few weeks of pootling around the waterways,' Nick said, watching the boat go by.

Ruth laughed. 'Did you actually say the word 'pootling?'

His eyes crinkled with good humour. 'Yes.'

'Deep down, you're a bit of a fogey, aren't you?' she teased him.

He began to object and then smiled. 'Guilty as charged. I'm looking forward to retirement, a pipe, and slippers.'

'Oh God, you're not even forty,' she chuckled.

She spotted the buttons beside the front door to the building and pressed the buzzer for number 14.

After a second, the entry phone crackled.

'Hello?' said a male voice.

'Hi, this is North Wales Police,' Ruth said. 'We're looking for Wayne Braddock.'

'Right … erm … he's not here,' the voice said. 'Hang on a second.'

A moment later, the door was opened by a man in his 20s. He had ginger hair, a short beard, and was wearing a green Reading University hoodie and grey joggers.

He gave them a quizzical look. 'I'm Sean. I'm Wayne's flatmate. Is everything all right?'

Nick ignored the question and asked, 'Do you know where Wayne is?'

Sean shook his head. 'No, he went out after work last night but I haven't heard from him. He's not answering his phone.'

Ruth detected that he had a slight London accent – or 'estuary accent' as they seemed to call it these days. She gestured to the stairs. 'Mind if we come in for a minute?'

'Oh, right, of course.' He opened the door wider so that they could come into the entrance lobby of the building. 'It's just up here,' he said, pointing to the stairs.

The lobby and stairs were clean and functional, and their shoes echoed as they went up the staircase.

Sean led them into a flat and closed the door. The flat was spacious, tidy, and fashionably decorated. There was a signed and framed Wrexham FC shirt up on the wall of the hallway, along with coats and jackets that were hung on a small row of hooks.

'Erm, would you like something … coffee or tea?' he asked. He was starting to look very flustered.

'We're fine thanks,' Nick replied politely.

Sean took them through to a living room which was less tidy. A few empty beer cans and a takeaway pizza box were strewn on the table. There was a large smart TV mounted on the wall, and a PlayStation games console and controllers on the floor.

'Sorry, I haven't had a chance to clear up,' he apologised, as Ruth went and sat down on the sofa.

You should see some of the places we go to, she thought to herself ironically.

Nick wandered over to a small set of shelves in the far corner of the room which had a few books and some framed photos on them.

Sean went and sat down in an armchair and looked at Ruth. 'Is everything all right?' he asked with a concerned expression.

'Can you tell us the last time you had contact with Wayne?' she asked.

'He sent me a text last night. He'd gone out for a drink after work,' he explained.

'But he didn't come back here later?'

'No,' he said as he sat forward. He was becoming increasingly jittery.

Ruth gave him a curious look. 'Is that unusual?'

'Erm, well, I just thought he'd hooked up … you know.'

Ruth assumed that by *hooked up* he meant that Wayne had gone home with a young woman or man.

'But he had work today. And he always comes back

here for a shower and to change but he hasn't been home. Has something happened to him?' Sean sounded genuinely concerned.

Nick walked across the room holding a framed photograph. 'Boss,' he said, as he turned the photograph for her to look at.

The image showed Sean in a bar with his arm around another man.

It was the victim from the towpath.

'Sean, is this a photograph of you and Wayne?' she asked gently.

'Yeah,' he replied cautiously. He already knew the significance of her question.

Nick came over and sat down next to Ruth. He took out a notepad and pen.

'Sean, I'm afraid that I've got some very bad news to tell to you,' she said softly. 'We have found a man's body close to here this morning. And I'm sorry to say that it's your friend Wayne.'

'What?' The colour drained from Sean's face. 'No. I don't understand,' he gasped. He looked horrified as his eyes roamed around the room.

'I know this is very difficult,' she continued, 'but I'd like to ask you a few questions.'

Sean nodded but he looked shell-shocked. However, Ruth knew that it was crucial to get as much information about Wayne, where he'd been and with who the previous evening, as quickly as possible. The first twenty-four hours of any investigation were the most important.

'I can't believe he's dead,' Sean said in a virtual whisper. He shook his head and blinked as he stared into space.

'I'm really sorry,' Nick said compassionately. Then he turned the page of his notebook. 'Sean?'

'Yes?' he replied, trying to focus.

'You said that Wayne went out for drinks after work last night. Do you know who he was with?'

'Erm,' Sean frowned and took a few seconds to reply. 'I'm not sure. People from his work. His manager, Gareth, probably. I know they usually go out on a Friday. Sorry … I …'

Ruth looked at him. 'Any idea where he was going?'

'Not really. We normally end up in Bar Lounge if we go out in town though.'

'Can you tell us what time Wayne sent you the text?' Nick asked.

Sean took a breath to try and compose himself. Then he took his phone and looked at it but his hand was shaky. 'He … he texted me to say he was going out for a beer at 6.30pm,' he said quietly.

'And that's the last contact you had with him?' Ruth asked to clarify.

'Yes.'

Nick scribbled this down in his notebook.

Sean then blew out his cheeks and his eyes filled with tears. He rubbed them with the sleeve of his hoodie. 'Sorry … I … I just can't believe this is happening.'

'Of course,' Ruth said empathetically. 'It's a big shock. But the more information we have about last night, the more likely it is that we can catch whoever did this to Wayne.'

Sean looked shocked. 'He was attacked?'

Nick nodded in confirmation. 'Yes …'

'Oh God,' he said in disbelief. 'Do you know who …?' He stopped and didn't finish his sentence.

'I'm sorry.' Nick shook his head. 'We're not sure at the moment.'

'Was he mugged or something?' Sean asked with a furrowed brow.

'Again, we're not sure why Wayne was attacked,' Ruth admitted gently. However, given the severity of the attack, Ruth's instinct was that he had been deliberately targeted.

'Oh God,' Sean gasped. 'How am I going tell his parents?'

Ruth looked at him. 'It's okay. I will be sending officers to inform Wayne's parents what's happened.'

'Right,' Sean said, still looking bewildered.

'Sean, can you think of anyone who might want to harm Wayne?' she asked. They already knew that Wayne had been charged with rape the year before and that the case had been dropped the previous week. However, Ruth wanted to see if Sean would tell them this and what his take might be.

'No. God no.' Sean immediately shook his head adamantly. 'Everyone likes Wayne. He's the life and soul.'

Nick looked over and caught Ruth's eye.

I wonder why he's not mentioning the rape case? she wondered.

There was silence for a few seconds. She could see from Sean's expression and the way he blinked that something had just occurred to him.

'Actually,' he said quietly with a deep frown, '… there is something now that I think of it.'

Here we go.

'Okay,' Ruth said in a tone that invited Sean to tell them more. 'Whatever it is, however small, it might be useful.'

'This girl had accused Wayne of attacking her last year in town,' he explained. 'He didn't do it. He's not like that. But it went to court. Then last week they dropped the charges.'

'And you think someone connected to this girl might have attacked Wayne?' Nick asked.

'Maybe. The girl's brother, Neil Watkins, found out

where Wayne worked. A few months ago, he waited for him in the car park. Luckily Wayne was with some friends from work, or I think this bloke would have attacked him. But he did tell Wayne that he was going to sort him out.'

Ruth and Nick exchanged a look. They definitely needed to find and talk to Neil Watkins as soon as possible.

Chapter 5

Ruth and Nick were in the car sitting in traffic in the middle of Chester. The sun was blazing down and reflecting brightly off the windscreen. Ruth leaned over and cranked up the air conditioning.

'Jesus,' she said, blowing out her cheeks and fanning herself with her hand. 'Is this air conditioning working because I'm boiling.'

Nick gave her a curious look. 'I'd say that it's verging on chilly in here, boss.'

'Right,' she sighed, 'another perimenopausal flush then.' The symptoms of the perimenopause were definitely getting worse. Her memory was shocking. *And* she was experiencing severe brain fog. The other day she simply forgot the word 'sandwich', and no amount of 'erms' or uses of the phrases 'You know' or 'It's a thingy with bread,' could explain to Sarah the word she was searching for. To say that it was frustrating was a huge understatement.

'Oh dear,' Nick said sympathetically.

'Yeah, well just be grateful you're not a woman and

don't have to go through all this,' Ruth said with a raised eyebrow.

'Don't worry. I know all about childbirth,' Nick said, pulling a face. 'Every day I feel glad that I'm not a woman.'

Before Ruth could say anything further, her phone rang. It was Garrow.

'Jim?' she said as she answered.

'Boss, there's only one Neil Watkins in the Chester area. He lives at 45 Princes Avenue which I don't think is very far from where you've just been.'

'Okay, thanks Jim,' Ruth said, as she tapped the address into the satnav in the centre of the dashboard.

'There's something else, boss.'

'What's that?'

'I ran Neil Watkins through the PNC. He's got a string of convictions dating back twenty years. Assault, GBH, affray. There are notes to say that he's a well-known member of the Chester 125 hooligan gang. He's got a banning order that prevents him from travelling abroad when the England football team play. He was arrested, detained, and then deported from Marseilles during the 1998 World Cup.'

'He sounds lovely,' Ruth said sardonically. 'Thanks for the warning, Jim.' She ended the call.

'What's up?' Nick asked.

'Neil Watkins is a seasoned thug and football hooligan with Chester FC.'

'Oh good,' Nick said dryly.

A moment later, the digital map showed that Princes Avenue was less than five minutes away.

'Go left here,' Ruth said, pointing to a turning.

As they turned, there was a sign for the Chester FC ground, Deva Stadium.

'Interesting fact,' Nick said.

'Another one?' Ruth groaned.

'Chester FC's ground is right on the England/Wales border, and their whole pitch is actually in Wales.'

Ruth raised an eyebrow. 'I bet they love having that pointed out.'

'Yeah, there isn't a lot of love lost between Chester and Wrexham football clubs,' he informed her.

A minute later, they pulled into a narrow residential street. The small semi-detached houses were built from red brick. The road was so narrow that there was parking only on one side with a double yellow line on the other.

They parked up, got out of the car, and made their way along the pavement to the address they'd been given for Neil Watkins.

Ruth's phone rang. It was DI Weaver.

'Hi Simon,' she said as she answered. 'I tried you earlier but I couldn't get through. I just wanted to update you on where we're at.'

'Okay, well fire away.' He spoke in a smug tone which suggested he'd found what Ruth had said vaguely amusing.

What's this bloke's problem? she wondered. *He's definitely overcompensating for something.*

'We interviewed Wayne Braddock's flatmate, Sean Lindley,' Ruth informed him. 'Seems Wayne went out for drinks after work last night.'

'Yeah, that's the picture we've got from his work colleagues,' Weaver said. 'We're just interviewing them to get a fuller picture of Wayne's life in recent weeks.'

'Okay … Sean claimed that Neil Watkins, the brother of the girl that Wayne was alleged to have attacked, had threatened Wayne a few months ago,' Ruth added.

'Right. That certainly seems significant. I'll track him down and interview him.'

'No need. We're at Watkins' home now, so I'll let you know how that goes,' Ruth said, making sure that she sounded helpful rather than pompous.

'Oh right,' Weaver said, sounding annoyed.

'I'll see you later then.' Ruth hung up and glanced at Nick. 'I think we're ruffling feathers.'

'Oh well,' he said with a sarcastic shrug. 'I don't think either of us are surprised by that.'

'No,' Ruth sighed and then joked, 'Bloody English, eh?'

Nick gave a dry laugh.

It felt strange to be forced to share the developments of an investigation with another CID officer like this. Ruth hadn't done that since she was a detective sergeant in the Met. And that was nearly twenty years ago.

They arrived at the address they'd been given. Compared to the houses either side, number 45 looked rundown and untidy. The garden was strewn with weeds, and there was a rusty old mountain bike propped up against a ground floor window. The once white paint-work around the door and porch was stained and peeling.

Ruth gave an authoritative knock on the door and took a step back.

Suddenly a dog began to bark from inside. Its deep throaty bark suggested that it was big. Its claws scratched at the other side of the door.

'He sounds friendly,' Nick said sarcastically.

No one answered the door and, after a few seconds, Ruth gave Nick a look. Maybe Watkins was out?

Nick wandered over to the downstairs window, cupped his hands, and looked inside.

'Anything?' Ruth asked. Watkins might be at work so their next job would be to find out where he worked. If he did work that is.

'Nothing.' Nick wandered back over to where she was standing.

Ruth turned to him. 'Doesn't look like he's in.'

Then there was a loud metallic clunk at the door, and it opened slowly.

A man in his late 40s, cropped black hair, tanned face, thick nose and blue eyes, peered out at them suspiciously. He was holding the collar of a huge black Staffordshire Bull Terrier which was barking and snarling. The man was wearing a sleeveless t-shirt, and his arms were full of tattoos. A large red and white St George's Cross was prominent among them.

'Yeah?' he said in an unfriendly tone.

Ruth flashed her warrant card and said loudly over the noise of the dog, 'DI Hunter and DS Evans, Llancastell CID. We're looking for Neil Watkins.'

'Llancastell?' the man said with a sneer. 'You're a long way from home.'

'Are you Neil Watkins?' she asked, ignoring his comment and feeling intimidated by the growling dog. That was the idea, she supposed.

'Yeah. What d'you want?'

'Can we come in for a minute? There are a couple of questions we'd like to ask you.'

Watkins rolled his eyes and then nodded wearily. 'Let me put the dog outside.'

He slammed the front door in their faces.

Ruth turned to Nick. 'You're right. Cute dog,' she said, with more than a hint of sarcasm.

'Cuddly,' he joked.

For a few seconds, they stood and waited for Watkins to open the front door again and let them in. He seemed to be taking a long time.

There was the noise of a shutting door from some-

33

where. It sounded like it had come from the side of the house.

Oh great, here we go, Ruth thought.

They moved quickly to look down the passageway that clearly led to the rear of the property.

A figure was running down the side passageway and towards the back garden.

It was Watkins.

'Shit!' Ruth groaned.

'For fuck's sake!' Nick yelled. 'Oi, stay there!'

They took off after him.

Ruth went into a full sprint, pumping her arms with everything she had. Since being shot and her cardiac arrest, she had been going to the gym and had started to run again. She was probably the fittest she'd been in about ten years.

By the time they reached the garden, Watkins was climbing a wire mesh fence at the far end.

He got to the top, looked back at them, then dropped down to the other side and sprinted away.

Oh great, Ruth thought as she grabbed the mesh fence and pulled herself up, trying to jam her feet into the wire. However, she surprised herself at how quickly she reached the top. Then she lowered herself down.

'You okay?' Nick asked.

'Just about,' she replied as they turned and continued to chase after Watkins.

Coming to a main road, Watkins tried to cross. He narrowly avoided a speeding car, and the driver beeped the horn in anger. Watkins then took off down the pavement to their right.

Ruth was now sucking in air as they continued their pursuit. Her chest was pounding.

Bloody hell, she thought. *I hope my heart is up to all this sprinting.*

Up ahead there was a huge municipal car park.

Watkins turned left towards it and disappeared out of sight.

Shit! Where is he?

Ruth slowed as they reached the car park, panting for breath, but Watkins was nowhere to be seen.

He can't have just disappeared into thin air!

Over to their right, there were two delivery vans parked up.

Ruth signalled to Nick that Watkins might be hiding behind them. She indicated that they should go around on different sides in a pincer movement.

Nick nodded to show he understood what she meant.

Ruth moved down the side of the nearest van slowly and braced herself in case Watkins had decided to lie in wait and attack her. She wasn't taking any chances.

She peered around the front of the van, her pulse still racing. But there was no one there. She saw Nick coming from the side of the other one. He gave her a shrug.

Where the hell has he got to?

Scanning the area around the car park, Ruth saw a series of large metal cylindrical bins. Thinking that Watkins could be hiding in one of them, she jogged over and meticulously checked them all.

Nothing.

There was movement over to the right which caught her eye.

It was Watkins.

Somehow, they hadn't spotted him. He was making his way casually through scaffold poles on the ground floor of a four-storey building that was under construction. He glanced around nervously but hadn't yet seen that they were now following him.

'He's there,' Ruth whispered as she pointed.

They broke into a slow run, trying to keep behind a huge lorry so as not to attract Watkins' attention and keep out of his sightline.

Hugging an exterior brick wall, Ruth glanced down the side of the building and saw Watkins now walking at speed towards a wooden fence and an open gate.

She looked at Nick and signalled for them to follow him.

Watkins was now fifty yards ahead, but they were gaining on him. He went through the gate out onto the main road, and then his walk turned into a run.

As they turned the corner, Ruth exploded into a sprint. Nick followed her.

Watkins turned when he heard the clattering sound of their feet on the pavement. His eyes widened as he tried to pick up the pace.

They were now only forty yards away and closing.

I'm taking you down, Ruth thought.

Thirty yards.

Ducking right into a side street, Watkins disappeared momentarily out of sight.

Ruth slowed a little as she reached the turning.

However, as she looked the side street was deserted.

Watkins seemed to have vanished again!

'Bloody hell!' she thundered angrily.

Nick panted. 'Are you joking?'

Ruth scoured the road and then noticed a doorway. She could just make out a fragment of clothing.

Someone was hiding there.

Catching Nick's eye, she pointed in the direction of the

doorway. He nodded and they made their way slowly towards it.

Ruth just hoped Watkins didn't run again. She was exhausted and sweaty.

Nick went ahead, and in a swift movement leaped into the doorway to apprehend Watkins.

'Come here,' Nick growled.

'Fuck off!' Watkins shouted as he wrestled with Nick.

Great, Ruth thought as she ran over to help.

Watkins punched Nick in the face, pushed him roughly to one side, and then broke into a sprint.

Ruth stood in his way.

With a nifty sidestep, Watkins went to run past her.

Yeah, I'm not chasing you again, Ruth thought wearily as she stuck out her leg.

Watkins tripped over her outstretched foot, sailed into the air, and crashed to the pavement.

'Jesus!' he groaned.

Before he could get up, Ruth put her knee into his back, pulled his arms behind him and cuffed him. 'You're nicked, dickhead.'

Nick looked down at her. 'Nice work.'

She puffed out her cheeks and gave an exaggerated sigh. 'I might be getting too old for all this.'

'Never,' he replied.

Chapter 6

The setting sun blushed flamingo pink across the sky, falling into a deep blue as the sea crept up towards the horizon. A swathe of tawny, rosy light lit up her face as she sat on a sand dune on Barmouth Beach. The sea breeze was still warm.

She took in a deep breath and smiled in satisfaction. It wasn't the sea or the breeze, or the soft sand beneath her feet that was making her smile today.

In her mind's eye, she saw his face.

Wayne Braddock.

It was that look of utter terror in his eyes that thrilled her so much. Revenge. It felt so just that he'd experienced that overwhelming feeling of terror after what he'd done. Men like him needed to be wiped off the face of the planet.

Around her were wild grasses that sprouted from the sand and then waved to and fro in the wind that rolled in from the sea. In the flat wet sand about twenty metres in front of her, three birds pecked and dragged at the bloody entrails of a dead fish.

In the distance, she watched a man walking along the beach with a dog. The way he walked and the way he was dressed reminded her of someone else from her past. *Kevin Green*. The man who had raped her and then raped and killed her baby sister twenty years ago. Her stomach tightened and churned at the thought of it.

She wondered if she would have been like this if Alisha hadn't been murdered? Other families got over such things, didn't they? They grieved but they also moved on. But Alisha seemed to haunt her. A blonde five-year-old too cute for her own good. She'd thought that before and wondered if it was okay to think such a thing. If Alisha had been a plain and ordinary looking child, would Green have targeted her? Probably not. But Alisha was the kind of child who everyone stopped and commented on how she looked. Like a little angel. Too cute. It made her jealous of her own little sister. All the attention, all that praise. But then she was gone.

Alisha had an imaginary friend. A giant stuffed giraffe called Gareth. But she called him *Gared*. It was cute. She admired her little sister. To have parents and relatives wrapped around her little finger at such a young age.

And then she was missing. And then she was dead. Brutalised in a manner that was inhuman and unimaginable. Her image all over the papers and the news on the television. It felt so wrong. Reporters and photographers outside their house for weeks. And then finally, she tried to move on with life, growing up next to the bedroom of a murdered sister. It felt so difficult. Well, not difficult. Heartbreaking. She used to walk into Alisha's bedroom. Smooth her hands over the white bed covers and look at the pink patterned pillow slip that still had a small indentation from her head. Her mother had laid out a set of clothes after she was killed, as though her sister was still alive and about to go out to a party. Violet-coloured dress, white tights, shiny black shoes.

It had been 5.30am on 21st July 2001 when she left the world. In a bleak, high place, battered by the sea wind. A lonely, deserted place overlooking the Irish Sea where the Vikings had landed nearly two thousand years ago.

What had happened to her little sister had made her so incredibly angry. Butchered by a monster. A male monster. But then again, *all* the monsters were men, weren't they? Men who preyed on girls and women. And it didn't happen the other way around, did it? Crazed, sexually perverted women didn't roam the streets at night attacking, raping, and murdering innocent boys and men. That just wasn't a thing, was it? Why not? She knew the answer. It was because men were inherently evil. They were programmed to act out their sexual desires with no thought of the consequences. They weren't nurturing, kind, or gentle.

Even the notorious women who had committed terrible crimes, such as Myra Hindley or Rose West, had been bullied and manipulated by men who were perverted psychopaths. Where did you ever find a lone woman who had gone out to rape or kill a boy or a man? Never, ever.

And that's why she was on her chosen path of righting the wrongs of her gender. It was war and it was time that women started to fight back. The men she hunted and killed deserved everything they got. They had already ruined the lives of the women they'd raped or sexually abused. And if they weren't stopped permanently, they would go on to do it again and destroy more lives. Termination was the only solution. Otherwise they would go on to have sons who would share their damaged, perverted genetics. And those sons would continue the cycle of male violence against innocent women. It had to stop.

As far as she was concerned, she was providing a service for society that everyone was too afraid to address. Men who attacked, raped, or murdered innocent women needed to die. And that was that. She was a walking death penalty.

It was a simple truth.

And had she not murdered Wayne Braddock last night, he would have gone on to attack other women. It was a mercy killing, in her eyes.

And now Wayne couldn't harm anyone else.

But the thrill and excitement she'd got from destroying him was overwhelming and utterly addictive. She wanted that feeling again. And soon.

It was time to find another monster to rid the planet of.

Chapter 7

It was getting dark outside as Ruth took a cold bottle of wine from the fridge. She poured herself a large glass of Sauvignon Blanc and headed into the lounge where her partner Sarah was sitting reading a printout. *Lose You Again* by *Tom Odell* was playing on the Bluetooth speaker.

Ruth slumped down on the sofa next to her. 'Hey.'

'Hey,' Sarah said, as she peered at her over her glasses.

The doors out to the patio were open as it was a beautifully warm summer's evening. Ruth sometimes wished they lived somewhere where it was always like this. Outside there was the sound of birds twittering as the sky darkened to a lovely dusky purple. The birds were what were known as the 'night singers' – the Nightingale, Song Thrush, Blackbird and the Robin. Then the distant chime of the bell at St Dunawd's Church in Bangor-on-Dee, which dated back to the 18th century, signalling that it was 9pm.

Ruth closed her eyes and let out a relaxed sigh. 'God, this is nice. Maybe I should have retired after all.'

Sarah gave her a withering look. 'Don't start all that again.'

'Sorry,' she sighed, her eyes searching Sarah's face. 'New glasses?'

'Yeah, well since you said my last pair made me look like Jeffrey Dahmer I had to get some new ones.'

'Oh, sorry. It was just a joke,' Ruth laughed. 'What's that?'

'Paperwork from the adoption agency,' she said softly.

Something about the change in Sarah's tone implied she was concerned about something. 'What's wrong? You look worried.'

'There's a section on health.'

Ruth shrugged. She was none the wiser. 'Okay.'

Sarah turned to her and raised an eyebrow. 'And there's a question about mental health and addiction.'

The penny dropped.

After Sarah's abduction in 2013, she had become a heroin addict while working as an escort.

'But you've been clean for eighteen months,' Ruth said calmly.

'It's going to count against us when we try to adopt Daniel,' Sarah said, now looking upset. 'I don't know why we didn't ever have this conversation.'

'We don't know that it's going to cause a problem,' Ruth stated, trying to reassure Sarah. 'The woman from the adoption agency is coming tomorrow night. We'll just talk it through with her.'

Sarah's eyes filled with tears. 'Sorry,' she muttered, wiping her face.

Ruth moved over and wrapped her arms around her. 'Hey,' she said gently, 'it's going to be fine. We're already great parents to Daniel.'

'I know.' A shadow of pain flickered across her face. 'I've tried to put that part of my life out of my head. And then when I filled out this form it all came flooding back.'

Sarah had witnessed a murder at an elite sex party in London in 2013. She was abducted from a train and taken to Europe where she was forced to work as an escort until 2020 when Ruth had rescued her from Paris. She had been diagnosed with PTSD as a result, but her medication for anxiety and some counselling seemed to have helped her.

'Maybe you should start back with your counselling again,' Ruth suggested.

'Possibly.'

'Or try NA again.'

Sarah had been to a few meetings of Narcotics Anonymous after talking to Nick about his experience of Alcoholics Anonymous. However, she seemed to think that she had used heroin to survive or blot out her ordeal. Now that she was back in Wales with Ruth, she didn't have any thoughts of taking drugs whatsoever.

There was a noise from the hallway.

'Hello?' Ruth said in a silly deep voice. She knew it was Daniel.

A face appeared at the doorway with a cheeky grin.

'Hey,' Sarah said with a smile, 'you're supposed to be in bed.'

He shrugged. He was wearing a black dressing gown that had an American football and the red and blue NFL logo on it.

He's sooo cute sometimes, Ruth thought. She knew that the teenage hormones were going to kick in soon and that he'd become monosyllabic.

'Can't sleep?' she asked, holding out her arms.

Daniel shook his head. She could see that he was hedging his bets on whether or not he'd be sent straight back to bed.

'Come here,' she said, giving in.

Daniel did a little run and jumped onto the sofa in between Ruth and Sarah.

'Aww,' Ruth said, hugging him and kissing his head.

'Aww …' Sarah did the same and they both laughed.

'Err, get off,' Daniel protested, rubbing his head, but they knew he didn't really mean it.

'How are the New York Jets getting on?' Ruth asked. For the past month, Daniel's new obsession had been American football. Several of his friends at school were into the NFL and they all supported different teams.

'It's not the Jets,' he groaned, 'it's the Giants.'

Sarah tilted her head. 'Well who are the Jets then?'

'They're a gang from *West Side Story*,' Ruth joked.

Daniel looked confused. 'What's that?'

Sarah rolled her eyes. 'Ignore her. Are the New York Jets an American football team too?'

He sighed as if that was a silly question. 'Yes, but they're mid.'

'Mid?' Ruth asked.

'I think it's kid speak for deeply average,' Sarah explained.

'Right, thanks for the heads-up. It's your birthday coming up, isn't it Daniel?'

He nodded.

'And you're going to be nine,' Sarah joked. 'I can't believe it.'

'Hey,' he protested, 'I'm going to be twelve!'

Sarah looked shocked and then laughed. 'Are you?'

'I've seen that there's an NFL game in London next month,' Ruth said.

Daniel's eyes widened and he nodded. 'The Jaguars are playing the Falcons.'

'Want to go?'

'Really?' he asked, unable to hide his utter excitement.

Sarah shrugged. 'Why not?'

He leaned in and hugged them both again. 'That would be amazing.'

Chapter 8

DC Georgie Wild went over to get the remote control for her television and felt a slight twinge in her tummy. There were still moments when she would forget that she was pregnant. And then something would remind her, and she would get the surreal thought that another human being was growing inside her. And that would blow her mind for a few seconds.

Now that she'd had a few weeks to get used to the idea, the anxiety seemed to have abated for the most part. Sometimes she was incredibly excited. But there were also times, usually around 4am, when she wondered what the hell she was doing. How was she going to cope on her own? Even though Pam and Bill had reassured her that they would be there every step of the way, it wasn't quite the same as having a husband or partner to share the highs and lows of pregnancy with and then bring a new baby home. And in those moments, Georgie would feel terribly alone and scared.

Putting on the television, she slumped down on the sofa. The news that Ruth wasn't going to retire from Llancastell CID was such a relief. Even though Ruth was her boss, they had become very close in recent months. If she was honest, Ruth had been a bit of a mother figure to her. So the idea of not seeing her every day had been a worrying thought.

Out of the corner of her eye, Georgie spotted something on the television screen. It was a reflection.

It looked like someone was looking in through the front window.

Her heart leapt as she spun around to look.

But there was no one there.

That's weird.

Feeling a little uneasy, she went over to the window to look, and then pulled the curtains. Then she headed out into the hallway, went to the front door and opened it.

The close outside was empty, and no one was around.

She closed the front door and locked it, wondering if she was just imagining things. Maybe the tiredness and stress of pregnancy was starting to get to her.

Chapter 9

'Aw poor little soldier,' Amanda teased, as she put an ice pack on Nick's swollen eye.

He shifted on the sofa where he was lying and winced. 'I did actually see stars.'

'Perks of the job,' she joked as she handed him the ice pack. 'Here you go, you can do that now. I've got to make us tea as you're incapacitated.'

'Shame. I prefer it when you do it,' he said with a smile.

Amanda leaned in and gave him a kiss. 'I bet you do.'

For a moment, Nick looked at her and was struck by how attractive she was. Her big chestnut-coloured eyes and tousled blonde hair. He was incredibly lucky for so many reasons. And while he remained grateful, he knew that his recovery from alcoholism would remain on track.

Amanda narrowed her eyes. 'You didn't really think Ruth was going to retire did you?'

Nick looked thoughtful. 'If I'm honest, I wasn't sure. And when I spoke to her yesterday she wasn't giving anything away.'

'I wonder why she didn't?' Amanda said with a quizzical expression. 'Good pension, lovely home, wonderful partner.'

He shrugged. 'I guess it's the buzz. It's all she's ever known.' He glanced at her knowingly. 'Don't worry, I'll be retiring as soon as it's a possibility.'

'You say that now …' she said sceptically.

He pointed to his eye. 'I could do with a job where this doesn't happen though.'

Amanda grinned. 'Maybe you should duck next time?' she chortled.

Nick's mouth dropped open. 'Duck? You cheeky sod!'

She leaned forward to get up from the sofa, but he took her hand and pulled her so that she fell on top of him.

'Hey, what are you up to buster?' she laughed.

He kissed her on the mouth. 'Fancy skipping tea?'

'Daddy?' said a voice from across the room.

It was Megan.

Nick and Amanda stopped kissing and looked at each other with amusement.

'Yes, darling?' Nick said.

'I can't sleep.'

He forced a smile. 'Okay. Do you want me to read you another story?'

'Yes, please.'

'I'll make tea,' Amanda said as she got up off the sofa.

He gave her a wry smile. 'And I'll go and read *Mr Tiggles Came To Tea.*'

Chapter 10

It was the following morning as Ruth pressed the button on the recording equipment and said, 'Interview conducted with Neil Watkins, Sunday, 8.30am, Interview Room 3, Chester Town Hall Police Station. Present are Neil Watkins, Detective Sergeant Nick Evans, Duty Solicitor Pam Sporle, and myself, Detective Inspector Ruth Hunter.'

Ruth raised her eyebrow as she looked at Watkins who wore an annoying smirk. His clothes had been removed for forensic analysis so he was now dressed in regulation grey sweatshirt and joggers. She had checked the national data-base, and Watkins' DNA and fingerprints were already uploaded from his previous convictions. From the notes that she'd read on the PNC, he was a nasty piece of work.

'Neil, do you understand that you are still under arrest for assaulting a police officer?' she said.

He shrugged and smiled. He seemed desperate to let them know that he wasn't remotely fazed by any of this.

Ruth fixed him with a stare. 'I'm going to need a verbal answer from you please Neil. Do you understand that you are still under arrest for assaulting a police officer?'

'Yeah,' he replied with a sigh as if this was all a bit tedious for him. Then his gaze turned to Nick. 'It wasn't really assault though, was it? I gave twinkle toes here a bit of a tap and barged him out of the way.'

Nick ignored him as he pulled a pen from his jacket pocket.

Ruth had arranged for a search warrant to be issued for Watkins' house, and a forensic team of SOCOs were going to the property this morning. She pulled over a blue manilla folder so that it was in front of her.

Nick clicked his pen open and took a pad of A4 paper so he could take notes.

'Can you tell me why you ran from us yesterday afternoon, Neil?' Ruth asked, in her well-rehearsed polite manner.

He rolled his eyes as if this was a ludicrous question. 'You're police officers,' he said, as if this was an irritatingly obvious answer.

Nick stared at him. 'And you run every time you see a police officer, do you?'

'Yeah, pretty much. I don't like coppers for starters. And I've been fitted up by your lot enough times for me to run and then answer questions later.'

Nick pointed to his face and swollen eye. 'And you make a habit of assaulting police officers as well, do you?'

Watkins smiled at Nick. 'Yeah, if I can.'

He's such a prick, Ruth thought to herself.

The duty solicitor leaned in and spoke to Watkins quietly. Ruth assumed that she was telling him not to openly admit to the assault or to try and deliberately wind them up.

Ruth shifted forward in her seat. 'Can you tell us where you were on Friday night, Neil?'

He didn't respond for a few seconds as he considered his answer. Then he said, 'I was at home.'

'All night?' she asked, sounding less than convinced.

'Yeah,' he replied. She could see that he was looking confused by the question but she had no idea if his uncertainty was genuine, or if he was faking it. 'Why? Where do you think I was?'

Nick stopped writing and glanced at him. 'Does the name Wayne Braddock mean anything to you?'

No,' he replied immediately.

Ruth shared a look with Nick.

Bullshit!

'I'm going to ask you again, Neil,' Ruth said deliberately. 'Does the name Wayne Braddock mean anything to you?'

Watkins put his hands down on the table and leaned forward towards Ruth. 'And I'm going to tell you again, no. I've never heard of him. Why, should I have?'

He was clearly hedging his bets and not admitting to anything until they told him what they knew.

Ruth opened the folder in front of her. 'You have a sister, don't you? Melissa. Is that right?'

Watkins visibly bristled at the mention of her name. The question had clearly rattled him. 'Yeah.'

'And Melissa was the victim of a rape in June 2020,' Ruth continued as she read from a document. 'Is that correct?'

'What are you asking me for?' Watkins narrowed his eyes and growled. He looked angry and uncomfortable. 'You've got it all there in front of you. But seeing as you asked, yes some vile cunt attacked my sister. But because you and the CPS are fucking useless, no one has been caught for it.'

'But Wayne Braddock was charged with raping your sister, wasn't he?'

A tense silence.

'Yeah, he was,' he eventually said through gritted teeth, 'but you let him go.'

Nick inclined his head slightly and asked, 'Can you tell us the last time you saw Wayne?'

'In Chester Crown Court, last week,' Watkins replied. 'Why are you asking me this?'

'And you're sure you haven't seen him since then?' Ruth enquired.

Watkins hesitated for a few seconds and squinted in confusion. 'Has something happened to that scumbag? Please tell me it has.'

Ruth continued. 'How did you feel when the charges against Wayne were dropped last week, Neil?'

'I was over the fucking moon,' he snarled. 'How d'you think I felt?'

'I'm guessing that you were incredibly angry.'

'Yep.' His eyes flicked from Ruth to Nick and back again. He was trying to work out what they were talking about.

If Watkins had attacked and killed Braddock, he was doing a very good job of hiding it. Ruth waited for a moment and then pulled out another document, turning it so that Watkins could look at it. 'For the purposes of the tape, I'm showing the suspect Item Reference 934G. This is a report of an incident that took place in the Watergate Street car park in March of this year. Although no charges were brought, we do have an eyewitness statement that you threatened Wayne Braddock that you were going 'to sort him out.' Is there anything you can tell us about that?'

'I can't remember exactly what I said to him,' Watkins replied with a shrug. 'I was angry.'

Ruth pointed to the folder. 'Well, we have three witnesses who can verify that you threatened him.'

'So what?' he snapped. 'That horrible scumbag raped my sister. How would you feel if someone did that to one of your family? Or would you give them a pat on the back?'

Ruth looked directly at Watkins. 'Wayne Braddock was found murdered yesterday morning. We believe he was attacked and killed on Friday night. Is there anything you'd like to tell us about that?'

'What?' The blood drained from Watkins' face as his eyes widened. 'He's dead? I …'

Watkins was thrown by the news. The duty solicitor leaned over and whispered something to him. Watkins looked annoyed as they argued in hushed voices.

'I have instructed my client to respond 'no comment' to any questions about this incident. I wasn't forewarned that he was being questioned in connection to such a serious and separate offence,' she said.

'I don't need to do that,' Watkins said angrily. 'I had nothing to do with it.'

'You threatened Wayne Braddock several months ago,' Ruth reminded him. 'The charges against him pertaining to the attack on your sister were dropped last week. He was attacked and murdered on Friday night in Chester. And you have no alibi for the time of that murder. Can you see how that doesn't look very good for you, Neil?'

'I don't care. I didn't do it,' he snorted confidently. 'Charge me then,' he said defiantly. 'Go on.'

Even though she couldn't be sure, Ruth's instinct was telling her that Watkins had no idea that Wayne Braddock had been murdered until two minutes ago.

Chapter 11

Ruth and Nick sat on the right-hand side of the large CID room at Chester Town Hall Police Station. Ruth had seconded DC Jim Garrow, DS Dan French and DC Georgie Wild from the Llancastell CID team to work on the murder as their case load was relatively light.

Sipping at her coffee, Ruth noticed that Georgie, who was sitting next to her, was looking very distracted.

'You okay?' she asked quietly.

'Yeah, I just got a bit spooked at home last night.'

'Why didn't you call me?'

'It was nothing,' Georgie admitted. 'Just my mind playing tricks on me and me being a bit silly.'

Ruth placed her hand on Georgie's arm. 'You don't strike me as ever being 'a bit silly.''

'You'd be surprised,' Georgie said with a smile, 'but I'm so glad you're back and that you're staying at Llancastell CID.'

'Me too,' Ruth replied, 'although I could have done with a less dramatic first two days back on the job.'

'Yeah,' Georgie agreed. 'Never boring this job, is it?'

'No, never.'

Georgie gestured to DI Weaver and whispered, 'Nick tells me that he's been getting his knickers in a twist.'

'I'm afraid so,' Ruth said under her breath. 'I think he's being overprotective and territorial.'

Georgie laughed. 'Don't suppose it helps that we've come over the border and we're foreign.'

'No, I definitely get that feeling,' Ruth said. She turned to watch DI Weaver as he collected his stuff and headed over to the scene board that had been erected at the far end of the incident room. It felt strange to be just a partici-pant at a CID morning briefing. Ever since she'd arrived in North Wales, Ruth had been the senior investigating officer on all major incidents. And since the departure of DCI Drake, she had been head of CID. She certainly felt uncomfortable letting go of that control.

The irony was that for the whole time Ruth worked in CID in the Met, which had been nearly twenty five years, she had never headed a CID team. In fact she had convinced herself that she never wanted that responsibility. And when she'd moved up to North Wales she had no intention of taking on that role at Llancastell nick. But now that she'd made that leap, and she'd become used to taking the lead, it felt very strange to take a back seat again.

'Right everyone,' Weaver barked a little too loudly. 'Let's get going on this please.' Ruth wondered if Weaver's no-nonsense manner was for her and the other detectives from North Wales' benefit. The more time she spent in his company, the more she could see that he was a man who wasn't comfortable in his own skin. Maybe it was because he was only about 5ft 7". Although it might have been a cliché, Ruth had certainly seen the overcompensation of what was referred to as 'short man's syndrome'.

'Okay, so this is our victim,' Weaver said, pointing to a

photo of Wayne Braddock sitting in a pub, holding a pint of beer, and grinning at the camera. 'Wayne Braddock. Aged twenty seven.' Weaver pointed to an area on a large map of Chester. 'He was attacked and murdered on the canal towpath just here. We believe that he was killed between 10pm and 1am but I'm hoping the preliminary PM can narrow down the time of death a little. We're waiting for the toxicology report to see if he was drunk or had taken illegal drugs.' Weaver indicated the photo of Wayne again. 'This was a ferocious and unprovoked attack. The attacker hit Wayne on the head with a blunt instrument and then stabbed him at least half a dozen times with something like a screwdriver. And even though Wayne's phone and wallet are missing, I want us to assume at the moment that he was deliberately targeted. It feels very personal. He was an innocent young man returning home after a few drinks with work colleagues. How are we doing with any eyewitnesses, especially anyone who remembers seeing him walking along the towpath?'

DS Kennedy looked over. 'Nothing yet, boss. Media have been informed that we're looking for anyone who saw Wayne in that area, or saw anything suspicious, but we've got nothing concrete yet.'

'Thanks. Let's get any CCTV that covers the path he might have taken from the city centre to where he was found. Get on to the local taxi firms and the bus depot. Let's get any dash cam footage that might be relevant. I also want us to trawl through Wayne's social media. See who he'd been messaging or in contact with in recent weeks. And let's get his bank statements over too. What about tracking down his mobile phone?'

A male detective, bald, early 50s, looked up. 'I've spoken to digital forensics. Now we've got the number, we should be able to triangulate calls and the GPS to get some kind of location, boss.'

'Good. Let's see if we can hack into his messages too.' Weaver took a moment and then looked over towards Ruth. 'As I've explained, we will be working in conjunction with North Wales Police as Wayne's body was found across the line of the border with Wales. DI Ruth Hunter from Llancastell CID will be leading a team of her detectives.'

Ruth took this as her signal to stand up and address the briefing. She wasn't going to stand on ceremony. 'Okay, so we've been looking for a motive for Wayne's attack. In June 2020 Wayne was arrested and charged with the rape of Melissa Watkins. In March of this year, Melissa's brother Neil approached Wayne in the Watergate Street car park. After a heated argument, Neil threatened Wayne for the attack on his sister. To be precise, he said that he was 'going to sort him out.''

'The threat has also been corroborated by three of Wayne's work colleagues who were with him at the time,' Weaver added a little too eagerly.

Ruth continued, 'Neil Watkins has a string of offences for violence and has served time for GBH. When DS Evans and I went to question him, he did a runner and assaulted DS Evans. We questioned him this morning under caution. He claims to have been at home all Friday evening on his own so he doesn't have an alibi. And he didn't hide the fact that he was very happy that Wayne had been murdered.'

Weaver raised his brows. 'What did you think?'

'If I'm honest, my instinct tells me that Watkins had no idea that anything had happened to Wayne.'

'I agree,' Nick added, 'and he was far too willing to say that he was glad that Wayne was dead.'

'Really?' Weaver sounded doubtful. 'But he did a runner when you arrived.'

Ruth shrugged. 'Watkins is well known to the police. It's not a stretch to think that when two detectives from North Wales come banging on his door, he runs and asks questions later.'

Weaver pulled a face as if all of this was completely ridiculous. 'I'm sorry but given his motive, his history of violence, and lack of an alibi, I'm not sure we should be ruling him out on a hunch or speculation.'

The tone of his comment was pompous and there was an awkward moment of silence.

Ruth bristled. *Oh, fuck off.*

She wasn't about to be patronised by Weaver in front of her own officers and Chester CID.

She fixed him with an icy stare. 'I'm just going on thirty years of experience as a CID officer and SIO Simon but no, I don't think we should rule him out completely. That's not what I said.'

'Cock,' Nick muttered under his breath.

Kennedy had just taken a phone call. She looked over at Weaver. 'Boss, I think we've got something. CID in Mold think they've got an attack and attempted murder with the same MO from six months ago.'

'You okay to go over to Mold as it's your patch?' he said to Ruth in a withering tone.

She gave him a forced smile. 'More than happy. Come on, Nick. You can drive because I definitely need to smoke.'

Chapter 12

Ruth and Nick had crossed the border back into North Wales and were heading across to Mold, a small town around twenty-five miles to the north of Wrexham. Now that the sun had burned away the early morning clouds, the sky consisted of varying tones of blue. Gazing over at Snowdonia, Ruth suddenly longed for those rare moments she had found peace there. Sitting on a mountain top with Sarah and watching the clouds drive across the sky above. Or the sound of the waves breaking onto an empty shoreline. They were the moments where she had let her life mingle effortlessly with nature, felt the slow beat of her heart, and gained perspective on her very being.

'Weaver's got short man's syndrome, hasn't he?' Nick said, breaking her train of thought.

'Definitely,' she replied. 'He's obviously overcompensating for something.'

'Fuck him and his needle dick,' Nick said scornfully. 'English twat.'

Ruth laughed. 'Hey, I'm English, thank you very much.'

Nick smiled at her as they entered Mold, got to the main roundabout, and headed for the police station. 'Yeah, but I don't think of you as English. You're honorary Welsh.'

'Right,' Ruth said, raising an eyebrow, 'and that's a good thing is it?'

'Of course,' Nick said as he parked the car in the station's car park. 'You know what they say?'

Ruth opened the car door and got out into the heat of the day. 'No I don't, but I'm guessing you're going to tell me anyway.'

'To be born in Wales is to be born privileged. Not with a silver spoon in your mouth, but with music in your blood, and poetry in your soul.' He closed the driver's door and popped on his sunglasses.

Ruth gave him a wry smile. 'Yeah, well I was born on a council estate in Battersea. The only music I heard was ska or two tone, and there definitely wasn't any poetry anywhere, so come on boyo.'

Nick's lips creased in a grimace as they walked towards the main entrance of Mold Police Station. 'We don't say *boyo* in North Wales.'

RUTH AND NICK had been waiting in an interview room on the ground floor of Mold nick for about ten minutes. It was smart and modern in comparison to the rooms at Llancastell nick which was built back in the early 70s. The room was painted dark green, with a strip of pine running around the walls at about waist height and then white paint below that. The chairs were black, fabric, and slightly padded – much more comfortable than those at Llancastell. Up on the wall was a monitor and to their right, recording equipment.

The door opened and a detective walked in. He was in his 30s with ginger hair and beard, green eyes, and wearing a smart charcoal grey suit. He was carrying a couple of manilla case folders.

'Hi,' he said, approaching with a half-smile as he offered his hand. 'DS Aled Jones.' Then he grinned. 'And yes, I get teased about that on a daily basis.'

'DI Ruth Hunter and DS Nick Evans,' Ruth replied as they all shook hands.

He sat down and then frowned as he looked over at them. 'You guys work out of Llancastell CID, don't you?'

North Wales Police force wasn't that big, and Ruth knew the names of the higher-ranking officers at most of the police stations in the area.

'Yes,' Nick said. 'It's a joint investigation with Cheshire Police. There's a jurisdiction issue with where the body was found.'

For a moment, DS Jones looked none the wiser – and then the penny dropped. 'You mean the body was found in England and in Wales?'

'Yep,' Ruth replied with a dark ironic expression. 'If you can believe that?'

'It's a new one on me,' Jones admitted, 'although I think I saw a Scandi Noir drama that had something like that in it.'

'Right,' Nick said. 'Well, if it had subtitles it probably passed me by I'm afraid.'

Ruth gestured to Nick with a smile. 'DS Evans can't read,' she quipped.

Jones laughed.

'You think you've got a possible attempted murder that's similar to our case, is that right?' she asked.

'I think so,' he replied, as he reached over and opened one of the case files. 'Last February.' He turned a photo that showed a man in his mid-20s. 'The victim was Steve O'Connell. He's twenty-five. He'd been out for a few beers, watching the rugby in a local pub. As he walked home, someone cracked him on the head with something like a hammer. Then they stabbed him seven times. He lost a lot of blood and was in a coma for two weeks. But somehow, he managed to survive.'

'What did forensics think he'd been stabbed with?' Nick asked.

'It wasn't a knife,' Jones said. 'The surgeon thought it was probably a flathead screwdriver.'

Ruth and Nick shared a look. *This is getting interesting.*

'Yeah, that's what our pathologist thinks too,' Ruth said.

'Did the victim get a look at the attacker at all?' Nick enquired.

'No. But the attacker did call out his name before the attack as if they knew him. That's why he stopped.'

'Right,' Ruth said, thinking that this was very significant. 'That seems to confirm that it wasn't a random attack and that he was targeted.'

Nick scratched his beard and then asked, 'But he didn't recognise the voice?'

'No,' Jones replied, 'but he did say it was slightly high-pitched. Like it was someone quite young.'

'Young?' Nick said.

'Maybe a teenager,' Jones suggested.

'What about possible motive?'

Jones gave them a knowing look. 'That's the thing that made me ring you guys over in Chester. In August 2020, Steve O'Connell was arrested for attacking and raping a young woman at a house party just outside Mold.'

Ruth's ears pricked up at this. 'What happened?'

'The charges were dropped by the CPS two weeks before Steve O'Connell was attacked.'

Bingo, we've got our link, Ruth thought. It was virtually identical to the murder of Wayne Braddock.

Chapter 13

Ruth and Nick parked up in central Mold outside a large MOT and tyre garage where they'd been told that Steve O'Connell worked. Even though DS Jones had assured them that O'Connell had given them everything he could remember about the attack, Ruth wanted to double check. After all, he might have remembered something in the interim.

They got out of the car and Ruth squinted up at the cloudless sky. Taking out her sunglasses, she put them on and glanced over in the direction of the garage. She could see there were three bays where cars had been elevated so that the mechanics could get to the underside of the vehicles in the inspection pits. There was a strong smell of oil and diesel in the air, and loud music was playing from somewhere inside.

As Ruth and Nick wandered over, a bald middle-aged man with a paunch, dressed in oil-stained overalls, saw them and strolled over. Ruth knew that they didn't look like your average punters looking for an MOT or a new tyre.

And anyone with a bit of nous would suspect they were coppers.

'Can I help?' he asked warily as he wiped his oil-stained hands on a cloth.

Ruth and Nick pulled out their warrant cards. 'DI Hunter, DS Evans, Llancastell CID. We're looking for Steve O'Connell.'

'Oh right,' the man said with a withering expression. 'Have you found him then?'

'Sorry?' Nick said.

'The bloke that nearly killed Steve,' he explained impatiently. 'He hasn't been the same since, you know.'

Ruth ignored him and said politely, 'If you could point us in the right direction …'

'The first bay over there,' he said, sounding distinctly unfriendly.

'Thanks,' Nick said with a forced smile.

'You lot should have found him by now,' he called after them, but they didn't respond.

As they got closer to the bay, a handsome young man with straw-blond hair and a scruffy beard climbed out of the inspection pit and looked over at them.

It was Steve O'Connell.

'Steve O'Connell?' Ruth asked as she took out her warrant card. 'I'm DI Hunter from Llancastell CID. And this is DS Evans. I wonder if we could ask you a couple of questions? It won't take long.'

'Really?' Steve's face fell. He shrugged. 'What do you want?' he asked in a hostile tone. Ruth assumed that he felt he had been let down by police who had failed to find the person who had nearly killed him.

'A young man was murdered in Chester last night,' Nick explained, 'and—'

Steve interrupted him. 'Yeah, I saw that, but what's it got to do with me?'

'We think that the person who attacked you back in February might also be responsible for this young man's murder.'

'What?' Steve looked confused. 'Why would you think that?'

'I'm afraid we can't discuss the details of an ongoing investigation,' Ruth said gently, 'but there are a lot of similarities. That's why we wanted to talk to you.'

'I don't understand. What's this bloke got to do with me?'

'We're not sure yet,' Nick replied. 'We just wanted to see if there was anything you can remember about the person who attacked you that might help us?'

Steve looked crestfallen at the thought of having to go over all this again. 'Look, there's nothing that I haven't told you lot about ten times already. Don't you talk to each other?' he snapped.

'I know this is very frustrating,' Ruth said, trying to appease him, 'but sometimes a very small detail can be the key to finding an assailant before they attack someone else.'

Steve shrugged with a resigned expression. 'What do you want to know?'

'You didn't see anything of your attacker?' Ruth asked. 'Height, build, any skin?'

'No, nothing.' Steve gave a frustrated groan. 'They just called out my name.'

'Both names?' Nick asked.

'What?'

'Did your attacker call you 'Steve'? Or did they use your surname as well?'

'They shouted 'Steve', and then they said 'Steve O'Connell' as they came towards me.'

He was starting to look uneasy and troubled by having to talk about his attack again.

'Is there anything else you remember?' Ruth asked gently, aware that he was starting to look upset.

'They were wearing a dark hoodie, and then next thing they'd smashed me across the head.'

'And you didn't recognise the voice?' Nick asked to clarify.

'No, I didn't,' he snapped.

'But you did think the voice was high-pitched though?'

'Yeah,' he said with a nod.

'Possibly someone young? A teenager?' Ruth suggested.

Something changed in Steve's expression. It was as if something had just occurred to him.

'Please. Anything, whatever you're thinking, it might just help us catch the person who attacked you,' Ruth said. 'And murdered this young man last night.'

'It's just the more I think about it …' he paused, as if this was uncomfortable to say, '… the more I think it might have been a woman's voice.'

Ruth nodded empathetically. 'If you had to say one way or the other, do you think the voice you heard was a woman?'

Steve looked slightly embarrassed. Clearly, admitting that he'd been attacked by a woman wasn't something he was comfortable doing.

'Yeah, I'm pretty sure it was actually,' he mumbled.

Ruth and Nick weren't expecting that – and if Steve O'Connell was right, it was a very significant development.

Chapter 14

It was 3pm and Ruth, Nick, Garrow, Georgie and French had now ensconced themselves in a small room down the corridor from the CID office at Chester Town Hall Police Station. It wasn't that Ruth didn't want to be around the CID team, it was just that they'd been assigned a poky area over by the coffee machine which wasn't conducive to work. She had no idea if this was a deliberate attempt by Weaver to play silly buggers. She wouldn't put it past him. However, they'd moved a few tables and desks around and this is where they were going to base themselves while they were there.

French, who had rolled up his shirt sleeves and loosened his tie due to the heat, got up. 'How about I go and steal a fan from somewhere?'

'Good idea,' Georgie gasped. 'I'm melting.'

'While I'm out, I'll go to the canteen for a coffee run if anyone wants anything?'

Ruth fished out a ten-pound note and waved it at him. 'It's definitely my shout this time.'

'Sure?' he asked.

'I'll be offended if you don't take it, Dan,' she replied with a smile.

'Thanks, boss,' he said, as he took the note from her. 'Same again?'

'Cold drink please,' Nick said. 'Diet Coke. Anything like that.'

'Water,' Georgie said. 'Fizzy and very cold.'

'Right you are.' French headed for the door and left.

For a few seconds, Ruth tried to focus on what they knew so far about the case.

'We just need something else that connects these two men,' she said, thinking out loud.

Nick glanced at her. 'What if they're not connected?'

Ruth sat forward in her seat. 'How d'you mean?'

'The one thing that connects them is that they were both charged with rape, and in both cases the charges were eventually dropped.'

'Okay,' Ruth said, but she was none the wiser.

'Maybe it's just some vigilante out there who has read about these cases in the papers or on the news,' he continued. 'They've hunted the two men down and attacked them.'

Ruth thought for a second. 'Cases like this don't normally get reported in the papers. And I'm pretty sure that when the charges are dropped, that isn't reported either. Where would a member of the general public get this information from unless they were deliberately looking for it?'

Garrow signalled to them and pointed to his computer. 'I did a quick Google search just now. O'Connell's attack comes up in the local press, but the alleged rape and the fact that charges against him were dropped doesn't appear anywhere. The same with Wayne Braddock. I don't think either were widely reported.'

Georgie cut in. 'So that means we're looking for someone who worked in some capacity on both cases, doesn't it?'

'If that information isn't in the public domain, then yes,' Ruth agreed.

'Who does that cover then?' Nick asked, thinking aloud.

Garrow's brow creased. 'Police officers?'

'Except it's two different forces,' Ruth said. 'Cheshire and North Wales.'

'Yeah, but there is some cross over,' Nick said. 'We hear about investigations across the border all the time.'

'True,' Ruth agreed.

'It's also two different courts,' he added. 'Mold and Chester. So if we're thinking court officials, they would be different.'

'But the judges could come from anywhere,' Garrow said. 'Plus both the legal teams.'

'Good point,' Ruth said. She liked the way Garrow's mind worked. It was sharp and analytical. As she'd found out since his arrival in CID three years ago, what Garrow lacked in street nous was more than made up for by his sharp, penetrating ability to analyse the pieces of an investigation.

The door opened slowly and a face appeared with a quizzical expression.

It was Weaver.

Ruth's heart sank a little. She was getting into her stride with members of her own CID team and she didn't want Weaver to interfere.

'Ah, this is where you're all skulking,' he said with a smug grin. He'd been out when Ruth had decided to commandeer the room.

'It was getting a little cramped over by the coffee

machine for us,' she said with a forced smile. 'I hope you don't mind, Simon?' Frankly, she didn't care if he did.

'No of course not. But it's a shame,' he said, pulling a face. 'I rather liked the idea of all of us in one room. Pooling ideas and resources. Working as a team. I'm a big fan of collaboration.'

Oh, do fuck off, Ruth thought.

Weaver's comments seemed barbed, but Ruth wasn't going to rise to his arrogance.

'We think this attempted murder in Mold is linked to our investigation,' she informed him.

'Do you?' Weaver asked, looking doubtful. 'You might be wasting your time to be honest. I've just rearrested Neil Watkins. He lied to us about being at home on Friday night. CCTV shows him in town just prior to the attack on Wayne. I'll let you know how the interview goes, eh?'

Without waiting for a response, Weaver ducked his head out and closed the door. He hadn't waited for Ruth to feed back about what they'd found when they'd talked to Steve O'Connell over in Mold. Not only was it rude, but it was also unprofessional.

Ruth forced a smile at Nick to indicate that she wasn't best pleased.

'Do you want me to hit him?' he asked dryly.

She laughed. 'I'm not sure that your 12-Step programme allows you to hit police officers.'

'And your sponsor might have something to say about that too,' Garrow joked.

The door opened and French came in carrying cardboard drink holders. He came over and set them down. 'Here we go.'

'Thanks sarge,' Garrow said, as he tapped away at a computer and studied the screen.

'Weaver has rearrested Neil Watkins,' Ruth said to French.

'I heard,' he said with a knowing expression. 'I ran into a couple of uniformed boys that I knew donkey's years ago. They reckon that not only is Weaver a total prick, he's got some vendetta against Watkins going back years.'

'What about?' asked Nick.

'Watkins stabbed Weaver's kid brother at a football game about ten years ago,' French explained. 'The Weaver family are from Crewe, and his brother was part of the Crewe Service Squad. Some hooligan thing.'

'Yeah, they're pretty nasty,' Nick said.

'Anyway, Weaver's brother now has to wear a stoma because of damage to his bowel. And Weaver is continually looking to pin something big on Watkins as some kind of payback,' French said.

'Great,' Ruth groaned. 'And now he's found this investigation.'

Nick gave her a dark look. 'Doesn't bode well as he's taking the lead on this.'

Garrow looked over from his computer. 'Think I've got something.'

'Go on,' Ruth said dryly. 'We could do with some good news.'

'The woman that O'Connell was charged with raping wasn't attacked in Mold,' he explained. 'She was attacked in Chester. I've got the notes here on the PNC.'

The PNC was the Police National Computer which allowed checks to be made on a person's criminal record, missing and wanted persons, as well as detailed notes on actual crimes.

'Interesting,' Ruth said, although she wasn't exactly sure what it gave them yet.

'Gets better,' Garrow continued. 'A Sergeant Kelly

Naylor was the arresting officer when Steve O'Connell was taken to Chester nick in August 2020. I've checked the log. Kelly Naylor was also the duty sergeant at Chester nick when Wayne Braddock was arrested in June 2020.'

Ruth thought about it for a moment and sighed. She wondered if they were on to something. She certainly didn't like the idea that a female police officer could be responsible for the crimes, but they had to follow the evidence – wherever it led them.

'Where does Kelly Naylor work now?' she asked.

Garrow pulled a face and pointed to the floor. 'Here.'

'Oh good.' Ruth rolled her eyes sarcastically. 'That's going to go down well, isn't it?'

Nick turned to face her. 'What is it they say? Don't shit on your own doorstep.'

Chapter 15

Ruth and Nick had managed to track down Sergeant Kelly Naylor who had been working downstairs in the custody suite. She was late 40s, with blonde hair pulled back in a bun. Although she had remained professional when Ruth had explained that they needed to talk to her, it was clear that she wasn't happy about it.

They were now sitting in Interview Room 2 on the ground floor of Chester Town Hall nick.

Kelly sat opposite Ruth and Nick, making it very clear with her body language and face that she was not thrilled to be interviewed by CID officers from another police force.

Ruth took a breath and then pointed to the recording equipment. 'Just so that you're aware, even though this is an informal interview we will be recording it in case anything you say needs to be used as evidence in court. Do you understand that, Kelly?'

'Oh yeah,' she replied with an ironic smile.

'Okay,' Ruth said, feeling uncomfortable as she leaned over and pressed the red record button. There was a long electronic beep. 'Interview conducted with Sergeant Kelly Naylor, Interview Room 2, Chester Town Hall Police Station. Present are Sergeant Kelly Naylor, Detective Sergeant Nick Evans, and myself, Detective Inspector Ruth Hunter.'

Kelly sat back with a peeved expression and crossed her legs. 'I should have my Police Federation rep here really.'

Ruth glanced at her. 'As I said, this is an informal interview for now. As soon as anything does become formal, then I agree that you should definitely have a Police Federation rep with you. In fact I will insist that you do.'

The Police Federation was essentially the police's version of a trade union. A Police Federation rep was someone who would represent and advise members with their best interests as a priority.

Nick shifted in his chair and looked across the table. 'Does the name Steve O'Connell ring a bell, Kelly?'

Kelly thought for a few seconds. 'It does, but I can't remember why.'

Nick reached over and pulled out a photograph from a folder. 'For the purposes of the tape, I am showing Sergeant Naylor Item Reference 839K.' He turned the photograph to show her. 'Do you recognise him now?'

Kelly leaned forward, squinted and then nodded. 'Yeah. We arrested him for rape about eighteen months ago. We had to travel over to Mold where he lived.'

'Are you aware that he was viciously attacked and nearly killed last February?' Ruth asked, carefully watching Kelly's reaction.

She shook her head. 'No. Where was he attacked?'

'Mold,' Nick replied.

Kelly shrugged. 'Long way from Chester, isn't it?'

'But you were aware that the charges against O'Connell were eventually dropped two weeks before he was attacked?' Ruth said.

'Of course,' she replied, as if this was a stupid question. 'I was the arresting officer so I was due to give evidence at trial.'

'How did you feel about the charges against him being dropped?' Ruth asked.

Kelly considered her answer for a few seconds. Then she looked at them with a suspicious expression. 'Why are you asking me this?'

'If you could just answer the question please Kelly,' Ruth said calmly.

She sighed. 'I was angry. O'Connell was guilty.'

'You were sure about that?' Nick asked.

'Yeah,' she snorted. 'I'd seen the witness statements, and the interview with the victim. There was no doubt in my mind that he was guilty, but it's not my job to decide that is it?'

Nick continued. 'So, you believed that O'Connell's victim didn't get any justice?'

'She didn't,' Kelly replied. 'She was let down horribly by the system.'

'Can you tell us where you were on 12th February of this year?' Ruth asked.

'No,' Kelly snorted, looking amused. 'Can you?' Then her face dropped. 'Hang on a second, do you really think I had something to do with O'Connell being attacked?'

'Did you?' Nick asked.

'No, of course I bloody didn't,' she said angrily. 'I'm a serving police officer.'

Ruth could see how offended Kelly was by the implication. Either she was a very good actor or she was telling the truth.

Nick reached over and pulled out a photograph from

another folder. 'For the purposes of the tape, I am showing Sergeant Naylor Item Reference 840K.' He turned the photograph to show her. 'Do you recognise this man? His name is Wayne Braddock.'

'Yes,' she replied cautiously. 'Of course I do. He was murdered on Friday night.'

'Have you ever met Wayne Braddock?' Ruth asked.

Kelly sat forward in her seat and sighed. 'Yes. I know where you're going with this. I was the custody sergeant the night Wayne Braddock was arrested for assaulting and raping a young woman in Chester. And yes, I was aware that about two weeks ago the charges against him were dropped.' Then she gave them a disdainful look. 'However, on Friday night I was out in Chester celebrating my sister's 40th birthday. I was with about twenty people all night. And I was in a club until about 3am and then people came back to my house. So, if you're trying to pin what happened to Wayne Braddock on me, you can stop right there.'

Ruth and Nick shared a look. Kelly seemed to have a watertight alibi. Not only did they know that she almost certainly wasn't involved, but they'd also probably completely alienated most of the station by questioning her.

Chapter 16

Stepping out of the car, she squinted against the bright sun and put on her sunglasses. The thin and wispy clouds had transformed into a formation that resembled a fish skeleton. She wondered what it was called – if it did have a name. Then she wandered onto the deserted beach, the only sounds being the rhythmic crash of the waves and the howling wind. The familiar scent of salt lingered in the air. To her left, she could see the unending expanse of windswept coastal land stretching northward. A rugged shoreline where jagged grey rocks met deep blue evening waves. Below the tide line, dark green seaweed adorned the rocks like shimmering ribbons.

She checked her watch. 6.55pm. *Where is he?* She had hacked his phone expertly, sending him a flirty text suggesting a romantic walk on the beach. Connor Barnard. Aged twenty-eight. Arrested for the horrific sexual assault of a nineteen-year-old girl at a halls of residence at Wrexham University. As usual, Barnard had been released on bail and then, due to insufficient evidence, the charges against him had been dropped. She'd seen the gloating

messages that he had sent his 'mates'. *Stupid bitch was drunk.
And if you wear clothes like that, what do you expect? Can't say you
weren't up for it the next morning.* The messages made her feel
sick, and only spurred her on in her quest to rid the world
of these animals. Patting her inside pocket, she felt the
shapes of the screwdriver and hammer inside her coat.

Looking at the vast beach ahead, she remembered
being here as a child. The far side was filled with V-shaped
ravines, scattered with colourful stones and small pools of
seawater. Along the sides of these ravines grew an array of
flowers in every hue: pink thrift, mauve mallow, and white
sea campions. The water had carved out crannies between
the rocks, creating hidden caves to explore. One particular
spot showcased a magnificent arched bridge made of rock.
From the top of that bridge she had watched the relentless
power of the waves crashing against the confined space
below. The sound and sheer force were both exhilarating
and frightening.

To her left was the long, dune-backed sweep of white
sand that dusted this part of the coast. A wave raced
towards her feet and she danced and hopped to stop the
water covering her shoes. Soft ribbons of birch-coloured
oarweed, the local kelp seaweed, gently curled in the water.

Then she spotted a figure walking in her direction.

Here we go.

Connor Barnard gave her a cheery wave and a cheeky
grin. He had what were now termed *Turkey Teeth.* Not
because his teeth resembled a Turkey. It was a derogatory
term for anyone with bright white teeth that looked unnat-
ural, and came from the rise in Brits going to Turkey to get
cheap cosmetic dentistry.

'Hey, Daisy?' he asked, as he got to where she was
standing on the sand.

She smiled at him and nodded. 'Connor?'

'Nice to meet you,' he said, and gave her a polite kiss on the cheek. He had definitely overdone it with the aftershave, she thought. Then he looked her up and down, his eyes resting on her breasts for a few seconds.

Jesus, what a wanker.

'You look prettier than in your photo,' he said.

'Aw, thanks,' she said, playing along and trying to sound as ditzy as she could. 'You look nice yourself.'

'Thank you,' he replied, continuing to grin like an idiot. 'To be honest, I'm a bit nervous. I haven't met many people online.'

'Don't worry,' she laughed. 'I'm not a psycho or anything.'

'Phew. Thank God for that,' he guffawed.

Then she touched his arm. 'I'm only joking.'

She gave another silly laugh as she surreptitiously scanned the beach. There was a man with a dog in the distance but she could see he was heading for the car park and would be out of view in seconds.

'I thought we'd head over to those rockpools,' she suggested. 'I used to come here when I was a kid.'

'So did I,' Connor replied, but she could tell he was lying. She assumed that was his MO. Do everything he could to get her into bed and then never call again. And if she resisted, even rape her.

'Wow, small world, eh?' she said, meeting his brown eyes. He gave her a twinkly little smile. He knew that he was good looking and that made her hate him all the more.

Another covert glance and she saw that the beach was deserted.

Let the games commence, she thought.

'Thought we'd grab a bite to eat after our walk,' Connor said. 'If you fancy that?'

'Why not?' she replied with an innocent smile.

You won't be going anywhere.

'Just a quick question,' she said, raising an eyebrow.

'Okay,' Connor said with a laid-back expression.

She fixed him with a stare. 'You do understand that 'no' means 'no', don't you?'

A look of confusion crossed his face. 'Sorry, I'm not with you,' he laughed.

'If you're with a girl,' she continued in a deadly serious tone. 'If she's drunk, or if she's not, you understand that if she tells you that she doesn't want to have sex with you, that it's not really okay to force yourself on her and rape her.' She arched an eyebrow. 'Are you with me now?'

'Woah!' Connor said, as the colour drained from his face. 'Who the fuck are you?'

'Oh, are you going?' she said in mock disappointment.

He began to back away, looking nervous.

'Hey, I'm out of here, you freak,' he snorted derisively as he turned on the sand and started to walk away from her.

Pulling the claw hammer from her pocket, she marched a couple of steps towards him and then smashed it as hard as she could against the back of his skull.

It made a sickening THUD.

Connor made a terrible groan and then crumpled into the sand face first.

She took the screwdriver, pulled him over onto his back, and glared at him.

'No means no,' she yelled in his face. 'Why couldn't you understand that?'

He was barely conscious.

'Who the fuck are you?' he muttered.

Then she plunged the screwdriver into his chest. It hit one of his ribs and jarred.

There was now blood at his mouth.

She pulled the screwdriver out and rammed it into his torso again as if this would somehow diminish the pain that she felt inside.

Connor was spluttering blood, trying to breathe. She must have punctured one of his lungs.

She stabbed him again, her teeth gritted tight.

This is for Alisha. And for me. And for all the other poor women out there who have been destroyed by men like you.

He stopped gasping for breath and went still. He was dead.

Chapter 17

Ruth sat in the far corner of their temporary office at Chester Town Hall nick. She was craving a cigarette, but she couldn't be bothered to go and stand outside with a bunch of strangers. At least when she smoked outside Llancastell nick she could have a natter with the other outcasts. She was particularly fond of Sergeant Gareth Pope. Having just celebrated his 60th birthday, Gareth was a proper old-fashioned copper who had spent the best part of 40 years working in the Llancastell area. He'd admitted to Ruth that he never had any ambition to climb the ranks of the North Wales Police force. Like her, he thought that the kind of people who became top brass were often out for themselves.

The door opened, which broke her train of thought.

Weaver came in and closed the door behind him with quite some force. He was fuming.

Oh shit, Ruth thought as she got up from her desk. She knew why Weaver was angry and she wasn't about to sit there and take his bullshit.

'Can I help?' Nick asked in a polite voice that was clearly intended to be sarcastic.

Weaver glared at him and then over at Ruth.

'I've just spoken to Kelly Naylor,' he growled.

'Okay.' Ruth met his stare defiantly. 'We spoke to Kelly earlier and eliminated her from our enquiries. Is there a problem, Simon?'

'Problem?' he thundered. 'You've dragged a respected police officer from this station in for questioning over a murder and attempted murder. What the hell are you playing at?'

'I don't think I'm *playing* at anything,' Ruth said, with as calm a voice as she could muster. 'We believe that whoever murdered Wayne Braddock also attacked and nearly killed Steve O'Connell. We spoke to O'Connell who told us that he now believed that the person who attacked him was a woman. By a process of deduction, we were looking for a woman who had a connection to both cases. Kelly Naylor was the arresting officer when Steve O'Connell was arrested for rape. And she was the duty sergeant when Wayne Braddock was brought in here for rape.'

Weaver narrowed his eyes. 'So what?' he snapped. 'Is that it?'

'She knew about both cases. And she knew that the charges had been dropped against both men before they were attacked. That made her a suspect. She has an alibi for the night Wayne Braddock was murdered and so she is no longer a suspect.'

'That's a joke.' Weaver virtually spat out his words. 'You could have just come and asked me about Kelly Naylor.'

'What does that mean?' Ruth asked. 'We can't overlook a suspect because *you* think she's a good copper.'

'Christ, whose side are you on?' he said with disbelief.

'I'm glad I don't work in North Wales Police if this is how you treat your colleagues.'

Nick snorted under his breath.

'You think this is funny, sergeant?' Weaver sneered at him.

'No,' Nick replied. 'But with respect, I do think that it's naïve to believe that a police officer is above suspicion of a major crime because there's a perception that they're a decent person. I heard about this copper in London. Nice family man. Twenty years on the job. A popular officer. Served his community in Kent in the Safer Neighbourhood Team. Then got promoted to the prestigious Parliamentary and Diplomatic Protection Team. He was trusted with carrying a firearm. Then in March of this year, this copper called Wayne Couzens kidnapped an innocent woman from Clapham High Street and raped and murdered her, then burned her body.'

Silence.

Weaver shook his head. 'Don't you dare put Kelly Naylor in the same category as that scumbag Couzens,' he said angrily.

'I don't think that's what DS Evans was doing, Simon,' Ruth said sternly. 'The point he's making is that none of us is above suspicion just because we're police officers. As a police force, we have to be completely transparent.'

'Transparent? Jesus!' He glared over at Ruth. 'I think that any cooperation between Cheshire Police and North Wales Police on this investigation is going to be difficult going forward.'

'That's fine.' Ruth shrugged. 'I'm happy to act as the SIO and base the investigation back at Llancastell.'

'No chance,' he snorted. 'We're staying here.'

'Okay. But if I think that you or any of your officers are hindering my team's work on this case, then I'll be going upstairs to your super to have a chat about how your family history with Neil Watkins is adversely affecting your ability to work on this case objectively.'

'Family history?' Weaver pulled a face as if he didn't know what she was talking about.

Nick stared at him. 'We know Watkins stabbed your brother.'

Weaver bristled and visibly took a breath.

Ruth pointed to the ceiling. 'We can go up there and have that conversation with Superintendent Rickson now if you'd like, Simon?'

'This is bollocks!' Weaver snapped as he stormed out of the room.

A moment of silence.

Ruth raised an eyebrow.

'Boss, you are my new hero,' French laughed.

Nick looked over at her and smiled. 'I think we're on our own here from now on.'

Ruth grinned. 'I wouldn't want it any other way.' She turned and grabbed her jacket. 'Right, I'm going outside for a ciggie.'

Garrow turned his gaze to her. 'I'm sure you quit smoking a while ago.'

'Yeah, that was until some fucker shot and nearly killed me,' she said as she walked across the office, 'and I realised that life is short, and I love smoking.'

Chapter 18

It was evening and Ruth sat anxiously on the sofa next to Sarah. Opposite them was Susannah, a social worker who worked with the local authority adoption agency. Ruth and Sarah had spent an hour before her arrival scurrying around like headless maniacs to make sure that Ruth's house in Bangor-on-Dee was spotless. Ruth had checked and rechecked the ground floor. She had also checked that all the fire alarms were working and all gates and doors were secure. Even though she knew that Daniel was eleven, so not a vulnerable teenager, she wasn't taking any chances.

Susannah was in her late 40s with long blonde hair, a pointy nose and chin, thin lips and glasses. So far, Ruth had to admit that she had a nice calm manner about her as she continued to stress that the most important thing in the whole process was Daniel's well-being and happiness.

Pulling out her iPad, Susannah looked over at them with a half-smile. 'You don't need to worry. Most of the questions I'm going to ask will be fairly routine.' Then she looked at Ruth. 'And I'm sure in your line of work you're used to far more taxing situations than this.'

Ruth wasn't sure that she liked Susannah's flippant comment. Or maybe she was just getting oversensitive because she was so nervous. It didn't help that she hadn't had a ciggie in over an hour, and she could hardly wander out into the garden and light one up – she and Sarah had agreed to tell a little white lie that this was a non-smoking household.

'Okay,' Susannah said, as she tapped away on the iPad. 'So, I've had a great chat with Daniel.' She smiled at them both. 'He's such a lovely boy, isn't he?'

'We think the world of him,' Sarah replied.

'Of course you do,' Susannah said, 'and Daniel seems very happy here. He told me that he's doing very well in school. Maths seems to be his favourite subject.'

'I looked at his Maths homework the other night and I didn't have the foggiest idea how to help him,' Ruth admitted with a laugh. 'Mind you, it's a very long time since I did my O Level Maths.'

Sarah shot her a look, and Ruth realised that maybe flagging up both her inability to help Daniel do his home-work, and her age, wasn't the best thing to have done.

Susannah pointed to the screen. 'We've had a lovely report back from Mr Taylor, Daniel's form tutor. He says that Daniel is bright and very well adjusted. Mr Taylor also commented that you are both very involved as his current foster parents, attending parents' evenings and school functions.'

Sarah nodded. 'Oh yes. It's a very good school. And he's made lots of friends.'

'That's great to hear,' Susannah said in a positive tone.

So far, so good, Ruth thought.

'Just a few things about you two to go through now,'

she said as she peered at her screen again. 'You've been together as a couple since 2007, is that correct?'

'Yes,' Ruth replied. 'Gosh, that sounds like a long time when you say it like that.'

'But you're not married?' Susannah said with a quizzical look.

Sarah smiled. 'Not yet.'

'You have plans to get married?' she enquired.

There was a few moments of awkward silence. Ruth and Sarah had talked about getting married on many occasions, but for some reason they just hadn't managed to get around to it yet.

'Yes,' Sarah said, directly looking Ruth.

'Yes, we do,' Ruth agreed immediately.

'And neither of you smoke or drink heavily,' Susannah said as she read the form that Ruth and Sarah had filled out well over two months ago.

'No, we don't,' Sarah said.

Jesus, what a lie that is, Ruth thought, feeling a little embarrassed. Despite making promises to give up smoking, she was now smoking at least ten ciggies a day. As for alcohol, she and Sarah got through a bottle of wine between them a night. And often more at the weekend. So that put them well above the government recommended 14 units a week. Sarah had recently calculated that they often exceeded 40 units each a week!

'Good,' Susannah said, tapping at the screen again and smiling.

Ruth relaxed a little.

However, Susannah then grimaced as she peered carefully at her screen. 'There is one issue that I would like to discuss with you Sarah. And that's your addiction to heroin in the past.'

Even though she knew this was probably going to be an issue, Ruth's stomach clenched at Susannah's comment.

'Yes, of course,' Sarah said in a calm voice. 'What would you like to know?'

'You've been in recovery from drug addiction for 18 months. How are you finding it?'

Sarah took a visible breath. 'It was difficult in the first couple of months. But to be honest, since then I haven't wanted or needed to use drugs. And I don't find it a struggle in any way.'

Susannah nodded with an almost impressed expression. 'That's great. Good for you. And you don't work a 12-Step programme or attend any kind of support group like NA?'

'No,' Sarah admitted, 'but if I did feel I needed support then I would be more than happy to attend.'

'Great,' Susannah said as she typed something into the iPad. 'I think that's everything I need.'

'And how long before you can make a decision?' Ruth asked.

Susannah got up from the sofa. 'I'll make my recommendation by the end of today. And then it shouldn't be more than a couple of days.'

Chapter 19

It was dark outside as Georgie moved across her living room towards the large glass patio doors so she could pull the curtains. She moved her hand to her bump for a second. That afternoon she'd had a prenatal check-up at the Llancastell University Hospital, and the nurse had reassured her that everything was fine. Ever since the car accident she'd been involved in three months earlier, Georgie had been hypervigilant about her pregnancy. The nurse had also set her mind at rest, telling her that she could come for a scan whenever she felt anxious or thought something was wrong. She wasn't sure that was something afforded to every pregnant woman in the Llancastell area, but given that she was a serving police officer who had been injured in the line of duty, she assumed they were making a special exception for her.

For a moment, her eye was drawn to the sofa and she thought about the baby's father, Jake Neville, who had been tragically killed nearly five months ago. Despite the fact that she and Jake hadn't seen each other for years before that night, Georgie could still feel the pain of the grief when she thought about him. Jake had been an investigative journalist working on a story in North Wales when he'd been deliberately run off the road. They had gone out together during sixth form, but Jake had gone off to do a journalism degree at the London School of Printing after leaving school. Despite their promises to keep the relationship going, the inevitable breakup happened after about six months. They were too young, and there were too many temptations for both of them.

And then, just over ten years later, they had bumped into each other by chance in Llancastell. After a few drinks, they had spent a wonderful night together at Georgie's house and made love on the sofa that she was now looking at. When Jake left the following morning, she had wondered if they might have a future together. But he was killed on the way back to his hotel in Portmeirion.

With her eyes filling with tears, Georgie wiped her face and blew out her cheeks. It just didn't seem fair that Jake had been taken away at such a young age.

As she went to close the curtains, a sudden explosion of light from the motion sensors in the garden made her jump.

Bloody hell!

Even though she felt uneasy, she squinted outside through the large glass doors.

Obviously a motion sensor had triggered the security lights. The wind, or those bloody cats from next door again.

Just in case, Georgie moved forward towards the glass. She peered cautiously outside.

The light dropped again as the motion sensor switched off.

Must have been a cat, she assumed as she looked out into the darkness.

A second later the garden was flooded with light again, and where previously was just an empty lawn, a shadowy figure stood.

What the …!

Georgie shrieked and jumped away from the glass.

'Fuck!' she cried.

The figure was backlit. Georgie couldn't see anything but the outline of a person standing there.

Although she couldn't see their eyes, she could feel their stare boring into her. She took another step back from the patio doors, wishing she had some kind of weapon with her.

The figure, who was dressed in black, turned, sprinted and then leaped over her garden fence and disappeared.

'Bloody hell!' she gasped, her heart pounding against her chest like a drum.

Part of her was terrified. But part of her was angry and wanted to rush out to the street to pursue the intruder.

Before she could make a decision, there was a knock at the door.

Oh God!

The timing of the knock meant that she feared it was the man she had just seen in her garden.

She could feel herself shaking.

Marching into the kitchen, she grabbed the largest kitchen knife she could find and moved slowly towards the door.

The person knocked again.

Shit.

Her mouth was dry and she took a deep breath to try and compose herself.

'Who is it?' she shouted, trying to sound as confident and strong as she could, even though the knife was shaking in her hand.

'Georgie?' called a voice.

It was Nick.

'Are you all right?' he asked, sounding a little concerned.

'Jesus Christ,' she gasped as she let out an audible sigh of relief.

Opening the door, she saw Nick and Amanda standing on the doorstep giving her a quizzical look.

'Hi.' Nick was holding a Moses basket with a blue fabric cover in his hand. 'I said I'd drop this round and …' Then he clocked that Georgie was holding a knife. 'Bloody hell. Are you all right?' he asked, looking immediately worried.

She shook her head, but it was all too much for her and she burst into tears.

'Oh my God,' Amanda said as they went in.

'There was someone in my garden,' she wept. 'A man looking in at me.'

Amanda gave her a hug. 'That's terrible.'

'Where is he now?' Nick asked, sounding very concerned as he put down the Moses basket.

'He jumped over the fence,' Georgie mumbled as she wiped her face and pulled herself together. 'Sorry, I …'

'God, don't apologise,' Amanda reassured her as Nick marched into her living room.

'Out here?' He pointed to the patio doors as they followed him into the room.

'Yes,' Georgie said.

He pulled open the doors and went outside. He looked around for a few seconds and then came back.

'I can't see anyone,' he reassured her, 'and there wasn't anyone out on the road when we arrived.'

'I'm sure he's long gone,' Georgie said as her pulse started to slow. 'I just don't want him to come back.'

Chapter 20

It had been 4am when Ruth got the call to say that the body of a young man had been found on the beach over at Barmouth. Nick parked in the car park alongside two patrol cars.

Barmouth was a seaside town that lay on the west coast of Wales about sixty miles due west of Llancastell. It was positioned on the estuary of the Afon Mawddach and Cardigan Bay, and although it had built up around ship-building, it was now a popular seaside resort for people in North Wales, North West England, and even the Midlands.

Although they had no details yet, Ruth and Nick wondered on their journey if the death was at all connected to their ongoing investigation. Getting out of the car, they retrieved their torches and made their way down a sandy footpath towards the beach. They heard the deep thundering sound of the black and yellow police EC145 helicopter as it swooped overhead and then hovered over the beach to their right, its huge searchlight cutting through the darkness to the ground below. There were already uniformed officers on the beach, and the SOCO van had parked on the sand.

'I haven't been here since I was a kid,' Nick said as they walked. 'My dad would drive me all the way out here. We'd spend about ten minutes on the beach and then he'd say, 'Come on lad, I'm thirsty,' and we'd spend two hours sitting outside one of those pubs.' He pointed back to the road. 'He'd get pissed. I'd have a few bottles of pop and some crisps and then we'd drive home. I wasn't really sure why we'd driven all that way to sit outside a pub but my dad's an alchy.'

'When I was young, kids weren't even allowed in pubs,' Ruth said. 'Me and Sarah went for Sunday lunch the other day and the place was heaving with kids running about. Like a bloody crèche. It was horrible.'

The moon was bright over the black water. Ruth looked down as her boots made tiny splashes in the shallow rivulets of water that criss-crossed the illuminated beach.

As they got further onto the beach itself, they saw the grisly sight of a forensics tent which had been erected over the body. The scene was lit by huge halogen arc lights, which turned the area into virtual daylight. The deep rumble of a diesel-powered generator filled the air, competing with the noise of the helicopter, and white figures of the SOCOs in their forensic suits moved to and fro as the lines of blue police tape fluttered in the sea breeze.

Two uniformed officers in hi-vis jackets were stationed at the rocky outcrop down to the beach itself.

Ruth took out her warrant card as they approached one of the uniformed officers who was holding a clipboard on which she was recording a scene log. 'DI Hunter and DS Evans, Llancastell CID,' she explained, as the officer scribbled down their names by torchlight.

'Thank you, ma'am,' she said. In her twenties, she had auburn hair pulled back from a round face.

'Were you first on scene?' Ruth asked, raising her voice against the battering wind that was coming in from the sea.

She nodded. 'We got here just after the victim was discovered.'

'Okay, thank you, constable.'

Ruth and Nick began to tread carefully over the rocks that led down to the next section of the beach. The rocks were covered in dark seaweed.

Looking up, Ruth spotted Professor Sophie Burnham, one of North Wales' chief pathologists, coming out of the forensic tent dressed in a white nitrile forensic suit and white rubber boots. She could also see that the SOCOs had laid down a series of aluminium stepping plates to preserve the sand around the crime scene for footprints and forensic evidence.

Burnham came over and pulled down her forensic mask. 'DI Hunter, it's been a while. How are you doing?' she asked in a concerned tone. She was clearly referring to the incident where Ruth had been shot nearly four months ago.

'I'm fine thanks,' Ruth reassured her. 'What have we got?'

'Male, 20s. Multiple stab wounds, blunt force trauma to the back of the skull. The victim will be taken to Llancastell University Hospital, so it will be Professor Amis who carries out the post-mortem.'

Nick nodded with a knowing expression. 'Yeah, we know Professor Amis.'

'Any ID for the victim?' Ruth asked.

'Nothing at the moment. No wallet and no phone I'm afraid.'

Ruth pointed to the tent. 'I think we should take a closer look.'

'Of course,' she said.

They made their way across the sand just as the tent was lit up with a sudden burst of light as a SOCO leaned in to take a photograph.

Ruth and Nick were handed suits, masks, and boots to wear. Once everything was on, they stepped inside the tent. A SOCO was taking another photograph – the flash further illuminating the material of the tent for a millisecond – and as he moved out of Ruth's way, she allowed her eyes to rest on the young man's body.

He was in his 20s and dressed in smart, expensive-looking clothes. His skin had a grey-blue tinge, and his hair was dishevelled and sprinkled with sand. Thankfully, his eyes were closed.

Ruth crouched on her haunches and gazed at the young man's face. He was handsome and well groomed. In terms of profile, he was very similar to Wayne Braddock.

She looked at the patches of blood where he had been stabbed - in his arm, shoulder, chest and neck. The attack was identical to Wayne Braddock and Steve O'Connell.

Ruth then noticed something in the victim's shirt pocket. Taking a pen, she carefully fished it out. It was a scrap of paper. On it was scribbled *Connor Barnard – 07804 365322.*

'What is it?' Nick asked.

Ruth showed him the paper. 'A name and a phone number. Might be our victim.'

'I can check that number in a minute,' he said.

Ruth gestured to the young man and gave Nick a dark look. 'I think we've got another one.'

He nodded in agreement. 'I think you're right.'

Chapter 21

'The sun is out, the sky is blue, but it's raining, raining in my heart.'
Who sang that? she wondered as she sat up on the dunes of
Barmouth Beach in the darkness watching the gloriously
grisly scene unfold. Roy Orbison or Buddy Holly. She
remembered that her taid used to sing it in the car.

She felt so utterly powerful as the police helicopter
hovered noisily overhead. Down on the beach, there was
an illuminated white forensic tent over Connor Barnard's
body. Forensic officers and CID officers were scuttling
around, talking, taking photos. The usual routine. This was
all her work. She didn't know if what she had done – and
what she was going to do – would ever be appreciated.
Waging a one-woman war on the vile men who felt that
sexually assaulting and raping women was somehow
acceptable. That ruining a woman's life forever was okay
because they had decided they wanted to have sex. And
the British legal system was letting those women down so
terribly. She knew that only 3% of reported rape cases ever
went to trial. And even then, only 60% of those men were

actually convicted. Technically that meant that for every 100 women who reported that they had been raped, less than two of those men would ever go to prison for that crime. It was utterly disgusting. And no one was doing anything about it.

Until now.

It was all very well having 'reclaim the streets' marches, but until these men were stopped and made an example of, women in Britain would have to carry rape alarms, get taxis, stay in groups or be walked home. Why should a woman walking at night be terrified of being attacked by a man? Did any of this work the other way around? Did men ever fear being attacked by a woman?

Never!

Well, now they would.

She wanted every man in the area who had a sexual assault or rape charge dropped against them to continually live in fear. She wanted them to be constantly checking over their shoulder in case someone was waiting to attack and kill them. And then, for once, the men of Cheshire and North Wales would get a glimpse of what it felt like to be a woman.

The wind picked up and blew around her face. Taking her hair, she retied it into a ponytail. Then, the moment she had been waiting for. The arrival of the coroner with a black body bag to transport Connor Barnard away to the nearest mortuary slab. There would be many who would agree that it was no more than he deserved.

However, she also felt a little pang of anxiety. She knew that she needed to speed up the frequency of her attacks. It wouldn't be long before CID officers began to narrow down who could have such detailed knowledge of these men's crimes, and the failure of the legal system to bring them to justice. It wasn't information that was in the public domain. And that made her vulnerable.

So, she already had her next victim in her sights.

Chapter 22

It was 7am and Ruth had now created a scene board in the small office at Chester Town Hall nick. However, they still didn't have the details for the victim from Barmouth. All they had was the scrap of paper Ruth had found in the victim's shirt pocket. Now they were waiting for the check to come back on the mobile phone number that had appeared on that.

Georgie walked in, went to her desk, and sat down. 'Morning,' she mumbled. She looked a bit lost and tired as she began to log on to her computer.

Ruth went over immediately – Nick had already told her about the intruder in her garden.

She sat down on the chair next to Georgie. 'Are you okay?' she asked under her breath.

Georgie stopped typing. 'Yes. I'm fine, honestly.'

Ruth wasn't convinced. 'You don't look it. And I'm angry at you for not calling me.'

'I knew you had that social worker coming around,' Georgie explained.

'It doesn't matter,' Ruth said, aware that she sounded

much like a scolding parent. 'You can't stay there on your own if you've got some idiot lurking around outside your house.'

Georgie shrugged. 'It might have been a one-off.'

Ruth shook her head. 'And if it's not?'

'Then I'll take a very big kitchen knife and cut his bollocks off,' she joked.

Ruth pulled a face. 'Given our current investigation, I think we've got enough women taking the law into their own hands.'

'Yes,' Georgie said. 'I'll take every precaution, and if it happens again we can do something about it. I'll be very careful.'

'Okay,' Ruth replied. The thought of Georgie being pregnant and on her own in her house with a possible stalker still made her feel very uneasy. As she got up, she put a reassuring hand on Georgie's shoulder. 'I'm always at the end of the phone and I can get to yours in ten minutes.'

'Thanks.' Georgie gave Ruth a kind smile. 'That does make me feel better knowing that.'

Ruth walked slowly over to the scene board and then looked out at her select team of detectives.

'Right, guys,' she said, 'we have another victim. At the moment, we don't have confirmation of his identity … Nick?'

Nick took a few seconds to think and then said, 'Everything about the victim from last night matches the other two attacks. It's the same MO and so we're working on the assumption that it's the same killer.'

MO stood for *Modus Operandi*. Literally translated it meant a distinct pattern or method of operation. In police terms, it was an indication that the same criminal was responsible for more than one crime because of the similarities.

Garrow frowned. 'I'm wondering what the victim was doing on the beach on his own.'

Nick raised an eyebrow. 'If we think that our killer is a woman, maybe she'd arranged to meet our victim there?'

'An online dating site?' French suggested.

'Maybe,' Georgie said, 'but if they'd registered for a dating site, our killer could be traced. Even if they were using a false identity, our digital forensics team could trace the IP address. It seems to be too big a risk for them to take.'

'True,' Nick agreed.

'I'm also assuming that, like our other victims, he was cleared of some kind of sexual assault against a woman recently,' Ruth said.

'Unfortunately, we don't know that yet,' Nick added.

Garrow raised a hand to attract Ruth's attention. 'Do you want me to trawl through the court records to see if I can find anything, boss?'

'Please,' she answered with an affirmative nod. 'The only Crown Court that would deal with something like that is Mold, but you could look at Wrexham in case it's a lesser offence. See if charges for a prosecution of that kind have been dropped in the past few weeks.'

'What about Nina Taylor at the North Wales CPS?' Nick suggested.

'Yes,' Ruth agreed. She didn't know why she hadn't thought of Nina Taylor already. She had been their contact point for the North Wales' CPS for several years.

'I'll give her a ring,' he said. 'Maybe she can come in and we can run what we've got past her?'

'Good idea,' Ruth agreed.

'Boss,' Garrow said as he pointed to his computer screen.

'Go on,' Ruth replied, hoping that what he had found was significant.

'Connor Barnard was charged with the assault and rape of a nineteen-year-old student in the halls of residence at the University in Wrexham in December 2020. The case was dropped by the CPS before it went to Mold Crown Court.'

'I don't suppose there's a photo of him?' Ruth asked hopefully.

'No, I'm afraid not,' Garrow replied, shaking his head.

Nick folded his arms across his chest and leaned back in his chair. 'When were the charges finally dropped, Jim?'

Garrow gave him a meaningful look. 'Last week, sarge.'

'Jesus,' French said under his breath.

'It has to be our victim,' Nick said.

'It's identical to the two others,' Ruth agreed, thinking out loud. 'Jim, if you look on the PNC could there be a photo of this Connor Barnard on there? We need to confirm whether or not he is actually the victim we saw on the beach at Barmouth earlier.'

A few seconds later, Garrow turned his computer screen to face the others.

There was a police photo of a young man taken in a custody suite.

'Yeah, that's him,' Nick said with a nod.

Ruth agreed. It was definitely Connor Barnard.

And now it seemed that they had a serial killer on their hands who was targeting young men who had failed to be prosecuted for the assault and rape of young women.

Chapter 23

Ruth and Nick got into the lift in the Llancastell University Hospital and then headed down to the basement where the mortuary was located. Ruth was frustrated at what had happened the previous evening with the social worker. She knew that Sarah's background and drug misuse needed to be declared. She was worried that if the social worker turned them down for the permanent adoption of Daniel, that might then impact on the temporary fostering licence that they had in place for him.

She tried to put her worries out of her mind and focus on the investigation. Half an hour earlier they had received a call from Professor Amis to say that he had found something 'interesting' in Connor Barnard's post-mortem that he needed to discuss with them.

The doors to the lift opened with a noisy shudder and they stepped out into the windowless basement corridor. They reached the double doors to the mortuary and pushed them open.

The temperature instantly dropped. Ruth got the

familiar odour of disinfectants and preserving chemicals. She remembered the first time she'd attended a post-mortem in the early 90s. Her sergeant had taken her along when she was still a probationer in Battersea. She recalled the shock of seeing the dead body of a young woman who had been kicked to death in a flat on a local estate. It had felt so horribly surreal seeing her bluish-white corpse just laid out on the steel gurney like a ghostly mannequin. It had taken her several weeks to get that image out of her head.

However, Ruth had soon grown accustomed to seeing dead bodies, and now she felt very little when she entered a morgue and saw a corpse. Once in a while, if the victim was very young, she found herself reacting emotionally. However, most of the time she felt nothing. She sometimes wondered if that was very healthy.

Amis was using an electric saw which squealed as it hit the body's breastbone.

Nick took a deep breath. 'Not sure I'm ever going to get used to that sound.'

'Might be you over there one day,' Ruth joked darkly.

'Oh thanks. Well I hope Amis has retired by then because he's very heavy handed.'

Ruth rolled her eyes, but the squeal of the saw grated on her teeth. There were still parts of a post-mortem that were incredibly unpleasant.

Amis noticed Ruth and Nick and turned off the saw. He pulled down his light green surgical mask and gave them a half-smile.

'Ah, the dynamic duo. It's been quite a while since I had the pleasure of both of you at the same time,' he said, smiling as if this was very funny.

Ruth gave Nick a withering look as if to say *here we go*.

'Have you missed us then, Tony?' she asked.

'Of course,' he boomed. 'You two are the originals aren't you? You know, it's like when Dennis Waterman left *Minder* and George Cole was on his own. It just wasn't the same ever again.'

Nick gave Ruth a quizzical look and shrugged.

'Before your time,' she said. She was impatient for Amis to tell them what he'd found that was so interesting.

Amis laughed as he reached over and took a mug of steaming tea. On the side was printed, *Do not confuse your Google search with my medical degree!*

Ruth smiled to herself as she read it. She wondered just how many humorous mugs Amis had stashed away in his office.

'What can you tell us, Tony?' Nick asked.

Ruth's eyes rested on Barnard's body. His chest was open, exposing his lungs and other vital organs. However, she could also see the red circular marks on the thighs, arm and neck where he had been stabbed.

'Cause of death is what I suspected,' Amis said. He then pointed to the various stab wounds on the limbs. 'All these injuries were fairly inconsequential.' Then he pointed to the deep circular wound on the neck. 'However, this is the bugger that did all the damage. It severed the carotid artery. He would have haemorrhaged and bled to death in less than a minute.'

'Anything else?' Ruth asked.

Amis went around to the back of the body, took a small halogen light on a stand, and moved it closer to Barnard's head. 'Blunt force trauma to the skull. Enough to fracture the bone here,' he said, showing them where the hair had been removed and the cracked skull was visible. 'The wound is small and circular, so I'd assume something like a claw hammer was used.'

Ruth pointed to the stab wounds. 'What about those?'

'Last time I saw something like those, the victim had been stabbed with a flathead screwdriver.' Then he pointed over to some notes on his desk. I've just got the preliminary post-mortem from the murder of Wayne Braddock from Chester.'

'What do you think?' Ruth asked.

'Same weapons,' Amis stated. 'And if you were to ask me, the same killer.'

Nick frowned as if he had suddenly thought of something. 'That's weird,' he said.

Ruth noticed. 'What is?'

'It's just that Peter Sutcliffe's choice of weapons was a claw hammer and screwdriver,' he said, thinking out loud. 'Might be a coincidence.'

Ruth gave him a dark look. 'Or someone might be acting as a copycat.'

Nick raised an eyebrow. 'Except the victims are all men.'

Ruth took a moment to think about this. She wondered if it was relevant, especially if they believed that the killer was a woman.

'Maybe that's the whole point,' Ruth said.

'How do you mean?' Amis asked.

'If we believe that our killer is a woman …' Ruth explained, 'then maybe she is preying on men just as the Yorkshire Ripper preyed on women.'

Nick nodded, then looked at Amis. 'Is there anything else that might help us?'

'Possibly,' he replied. 'Your victim was well dressed and covered in aftershave when he was murdered. And he had traces of phosphodiesterase in his bloodstream.'

'What's that in layman's terms?' Ruth asked. She had

no idea why Amis continued to tell them stuff as though they had a medical and pharmacy degree.

'Oh, yes. Basically something like Viagra.'

Ruth and Nick were both thinking the same thing.

'Sounds as if Connor Barnard was going on some kind of date,' Ruth said, 'and my instinct is that he was meeting our killer.'

Chapter 24

Having returned to Chester Town Hall nick, Ruth was now on a mission. She wasn't going to allow DI Weaver to use his bitterness towards Neil Watkins to screw up the investigation. She was convinced that Watkins wasn't involved in any of the attacks, but she needed concrete proof. Marching along the ground floor towards the custody suite, she saw a gruff-looking custody sergeant with cropped grey hair.

Knowing that he wouldn't recognise her, she took out her warrant card and showed him. 'DI Ruth Hunter. I'm based at Llancastell CID in North Wales.'

'Oh yes, ma'am,' he replied with a nod of recognition. 'I'd heard that there were some CID officers from across the border. How can I help?'

'I need to check on a suspect that you're holding,' she explained politely.

'Yes, ma'am.' He walked over to a keyboard and monitor behind the custody suite desk. 'What's the name?'

'Neil Watkins.'

The custody sergeant pulled a face. 'Oh yeah, I know all about Neil Watkins,' he said in a knowing tone.

Now that Ruth knew that their killer had attacked and murdered another young man, it couldn't be Neil Watkins. After all, Watkins' motive was Wayne Braddock's sexual assault of his sister. Ruth had already made it clear to Weaver that there was nothing to connect Watkins to the brutal attack on Steve O'Connell. And as far as they knew, there was nothing to link Watkins to Barnard's murder.

And if Watkins had still been sitting in a custody cell last night, he could hardly have been murdering anyone on Barmouth Beach.

'Is he still in custody at this station?' Ruth asked.

'We had to let him go about an hour ago,' the custody sergeant explained. 'Mind you, DI Weaver was not a happy chappy about that at all.'

'I don't expect he was,' Ruth said. 'Thank you sergeant.'

Ruth turned and headed for the stairs. It was time to challenge Weaver with what they knew.

Chapter 25

Opening the doors to CID, Ruth walked calmly across the office. There were various detectives working at desks, typing at computers, or talking on the phone. Several of them gave her a look as she walked by. She assumed that Weaver had been less than complimentary about her, especially when it came to the questioning of Sergeant Kelly Naylor. She could see how it might put their backs up if an officer from another force had questioned one of their own for something as serious as murder. But she had a job to do, and she wasn't here to make friends.

She spotted Weaver pacing around his office with a mobile phone to his ear. Arriving at his half-open door, she gave it a knock.

Weaver gave her an irritated look and pointed to the phone to indicate that now wasn't a convenient time for them to talk.

Ruth didn't care. She looked at him directly. 'Simon, I need to speak to you right now. It's urgent.'

Weaver rolled his eyes and then turned his back to her as she closed the door and then plonked herself down on a chair. What she was about to reveal to Weaver wasn't for the ears of the rest of Chester CID yet.

'Listen Peter,' Weaver said in an exasperated tone. 'I've got to go so I'll catch you later.' He then turned, went over behind his desk, sat in his office chair and glared over at Ruth.

He really is an immature twat.

'I understand that you've had to let Neil Watkins go?' she said.

'Yes,' Weaver said, and then frowned. 'I thought you said this was urgent. Is that why you've barged in here just to ask me that?'

'Watkins didn't murder Wayne Braddock,' Ruth said calmly.

'Oh right,' he sneered. 'Are we back to this assault over in North Wales again? Jesus.'

'It was an attempted murder that put a young man in a coma,' Ruth said dryly. 'But no, that's not why I want to talk to you. A young man, Connor Barnard, was murdered last night on Barmouth Beach.'

'I know, but that's two hours from here. So what?' he snapped before she could continue.

'Connor Barnard was smashed on the back of his skull with a hammer. And then he was stabbed repeatedly with a screwdriver,' Ruth explained. 'Ring any bells?'

Weaver shrugged but didn't say anything.

'And Connor Barnard was charged with the assault and rape of a young student at Wrexham University,' she continued, 'and then the charges were dropped by the CPS last week.'

Silence.

Ruth could see the colour drain from Weaver's face. He knew that he'd staked his reputation on his certainty that Watkins was guilty. He probably knew that his personal vendetta had clouded his judgement. And now he had serious egg on his face.

'I bet you've been gloating about that all morning,' he said snidely.

'Don't be so fucking childish, Simon,' Ruth thundered as she fixed him with an angry stare. 'We're working on several murder cases. And we might be hunting a serial killer.' Ruth got up and went towards his office door.

'A serial killer?' Weaver scoffed.

Ruth turned around, her face tightening. 'Simon, none of this is personal. I'm not remotely interested in petty point-scoring. But if we don't take this seriously, this person is going to kill again. And we need to stop them before they do.'

She closed the door behind her and walked across the CID office feeling vindicated.

Chapter 26

Ruth and Nick were on the outskirts of Wrexham, heading for an address in Gresford which was an affluent suburb to the north of the city. As they slowed, Nick indicated right and they pulled off the main road. However, there didn't seem to be any houses. Instead there was a small park with some trees.

Ruth glanced at the satnav and saw that they had taken a wrong turn. 'Yeah, we're going the wrong way, Tonto.'

'Actually,' Nick began, 'as we're passing, I wanted to show you something. It won't take more than a minute.'

Ruth gave him a quizzical look. She had no idea what he was up to or talking about.

As they came to a stop, he gestured to some kind of memorial to their right. It was comprised of a huge iron wheel. In front of it were two large, grey, stone plinths.

'It's the Gresford Disaster Memorial.'

Ruth looked surprised. 'I'm not sure I know about that.'

'I didn't think you did, which is why I stopped to show you.'

'What happened?'

'On the 22nd September 1934, there was a huge explosion and a fire at the Gresford Colliery, and 266 men were killed.'

Ruth's eyes widened. 'God, I didn't know that.'

'The English owners had taken short cuts when it came to safety and management,' Nick continued. 'The worst thing was, they only retrieved eleven of the miners' bodies. The owners decided to seal the mine where the disaster had happened and leave the other 255 bodies down there.' Nick gave her a dark look. 'And my great-grandfather was one of them.'

'Oh God,' Ruth said. 'That's terrible.'

'Yeah,' Nick agreed. 'Apparently my great-grand-mother never really got over it. And I guess that's why I have such a dim view of the English.'

'Not surprising,' Ruth said with an empathetic expression.

Nick gave her a half-smile. 'Except you, of course.'

'Yeah, well I've lived here so long,' Ruth said, 'I think I count as being a bit Welsh now.'

There was a poignant silence in the car.

Nick started the ignition and turned the car around.

'I just thought I'd show you as we were driving past,' Nick said quietly.

'I'm really glad you did.' Ruth looked at him. 'Thank you.'

Chapter 27

Ruth and Nick parked up in a leafy residential road in the middle of Gresford. To their right was a large detached house that had been painted white, and a sizeable garden with towering trees and neat hedges. There was a gravel drive with a black Audi A4 parked on it, and a double garage with painted wooden doors.

Even though it was the height of summer it was a little cloudy, but the air was still hot and muggy. It felt like a storm was brewing.

They walked up the neat garden path to a front door that had a black wooden porch and hanging baskets.

Ruth knocked on the door. She was already aware that Connor Barnard lived at this address with his mother, and that Mrs Barnard had already been informed of his death that morning by uniformed officers.

The front door opened and an attractive, well-dressed woman in her early 60s answered. However, from the haunted look on her face, Ruth could see that she was devastated by the death of her son.

'Mrs Barnard?' she asked.

She nodded but didn't reply.

Ruth and Nick showed their warrant cards. 'DI Hunter and DS Evans, Llancastell CID. We're so sorry for your loss.'

'Thank you,' the woman said in a daze. 'Would you like to come in?'

'Yes, please,' Ruth said gently.

'It's Charlotte, by the way,' she said as she opened the front door fully and let them come into the hallway.

The house was tastefully decorated with Farrow & Ball duck egg blue paint, oak furniture, and water colour paintings on the walls.

'Would you like to come through here?' Charlotte said, as she used a stick to walk down the hallway. She walked with a pronounced limp.

She showed them into a spacious light living room. There were two sofas facing each other, with a low coffee table between them. There was a floor-to-ceiling bookshelf at the far end, full of old hardback books. The air smelled of lavender and the musty bookish smell of a library.

Charlotte gestured to a sofa. 'Please, sit down.' She sat down slowly on the other sofa with the aid of her stick.

Ruth gave her an empathetic look. 'I know this is very difficult, but there are a few questions we'd like to ask you about Connor.'

'Of course,' she said with an understanding nod.

Nick took out his notepad and pen.

'How did Connor seem in the last week or so?' Ruth asked. 'Was there anything bothering him?'

'Quite the opposite actually,' Charlotte replied. 'Those ridiculous charges against him had been dropped. He seemed so relieved. That silly girl nearly ruined his life.'

Ruth bristled at Charlotte's description of the nineteen-year-old rape victim as 'a silly girl'.

'Silly girl?' Nick asked, looking over at her.

'Yes,' Charlotte said. 'I mean, I know I'm his mother. But Connor is …' Then she corrected herself, looking upset. 'Connor *was* a very handsome young man. He certainly didn't need to force himself on anyone. I don't understand why she lied about it. Maybe she was drunk or had taken drugs and then regretted what she'd done but she has made mine and Connor's life a misery for the past year. I thought he might end up in prison.'

Ruth nodded, even though she disagreed. Now was not the time to have that conversation.

Nick stopped writing and said, 'As you know, we found Connor on the beach over in Barmouth. Do you have any idea why he might have been there?'

Charlotte looked confused for a moment. 'Barmouth? No, I don't know why he would be in Barmouth. It's quite a long way to go, but I guess it's summer and evenings are long.'

'We think that he might have been meeting someone on the beach,' Ruth explained. 'And we think it might have been a date.'

Charlotte frowned. 'Why would you think that?'

'Just a few things that we thought pointed to that,' Ruth said, not wanting to go into detail. It didn't seem relevant.

'Like what?' Charlotte asked. 'I'd like to know.'

Ruth understood. Being on Barmouth Beach had been her son's final few minutes on planet Earth. Often it was a comfort to those who were bereaved to find out everything that they could about that time.

'He was very smartly dressed,' Nick replied.

'Yes, well he always was,' she said, looking a little teary. 'He loved his clothes.'

'And he was wearing a lot of aftershave and had

condoms in his pocket,' Ruth added, hoping it wasn't too inappropriate to disclose such information.

'Right,' Charlotte said. 'He didn't have a girlfriend. Or at least, not that I know of. I think he was still sewing his wild oats.'

'Is there anything you can tell us that might help?' Ruth asked. 'However small.'

Charlotte thought for a few seconds and then remembered something. 'Actually, a couple of days ago Connor did say he'd met someone. Or did he say that he was going to meet someone. I'm so sorry, I can't remember.'

'Did he say anything about this person?'

'Yes, he did. He said that I'd like 'this one' because she was very bright and went to university. I think that's what he said.' She lowered her eyes and a tear slid slowly down her cheek.

'Thank you,' Ruth said. 'That's very helpful.'

Chapter 28

When Ruth had returned to Chester, she had been summoned to the top floor to speak to Superintendent Ian Rickson, who was the highest-ranking police officer in the building, and therefore in charge.

As she got to the top of the stairs, Ruth noticed that she was a little out of breath. For a second, the little voice in her head said, 'That's because you smoke and drink too much,' but she wasn't in the mood to listen to it. Maybe she could address her lifestyle choices once she had retired. Whenever that was going to be.

Walking down the corridor, she arrived at the door that had Rickson's nameplate on it. She knocked and heard a muffled 'Come in' from the other side.

Opening the door, Ruth went in and saw Rickson sitting behind a huge desk. She remembered what an old sergeant had joked to her when she was in the Met – *Big desk, small penis.*

Rickson was in his late 50s, bald, with a chubby face and a goatee beard. He was wearing his uniform – white shirt, black tie, epaulets. His wide neck strained at the collar of his shirt.

'Come and sit down, Ruth,' he said in a friendly tone as he gestured to a padded dark green chair beside his desk.

'Thank you, sir,' she said as she sat down. 'How can I help?'

'Just a quick chat to see how you think this investigation is going down in CID. Obviously there's some media speculation, and I've had the chief constable on the phone.'

'Right,' Ruth said, trying to suss out why she was really sitting there. DI Weaver was head of CID at the station, so why wasn't he having this conversation with him? Or maybe he'd already spoken to Weaver, and he'd thrown her under the bus. 'How does DI Weaver think the investigation is going?'

Rickson took a few seconds to consider his answer. 'Actually, he seems to think that you're hindering his investigation by trying to link Wayne Braddock's murder to a murder over in Barmouth last night.'

'I'm not trying to link it, sir,' Ruth protested. 'There's no doubt in my mind that the person who killed Wayne Braddock also attacked and nearly killed a young man in Mold, and then murdered another young man on Barmouth Beach last night. There are too many similarities to even contemplate that it's not the same killer.'

'Right.' Rickson looked confused. 'Weaver told me that Neil Watkins is his prime suspect. Wayne Braddock raped Watkins' sister but the charges were dropped a week ago, is that correct?'

'Yes, sir,' Ruth said, 'but—'

'And Neil Watkins has a string of convictions for violence?' Rickson said, interrupting her.

'Yes,' she answered, 'that's all true. But the two crimes

I'm looking at in Wales also involve young men who were charged with rape and then the charges were dropped just before they were attacked. And my chief pathologist looked at the post-mortem notes on Wayne Braddock. His opinion is that it's the same method of attack and the same weapons as the murder in Barmouth last night. He told me it's the same person who carried out both murders.'

'I don't understand,' Rickson admitted. 'This is not what DI Weaver told me earlier today.'

'Sir, can I talk to you strictly off the record?' Ruth asked.

'Of course,' he replied, sitting forward on his chair. 'Technically you work for an entirely different police force in a different country. What is it?'

'Neil Watkins attacked DI Weaver's younger brother a few years ago,' Ruth explained. 'The attack left him with a stoma.'

Rickson shook his head. 'I didn't know that.'

'I can understand that DI Weaver has a grievance against Watkins, but I really do feel it's seriously clouded his judgement.'

'Yes,' Rickson said thoughtfully.

'Of course, normally I would have my colleague's back in something like this,' Ruth explained, 'but we're looking for someone who is incredibly dangerous. We can't afford to make any mistakes.'

'No, quite,' Rickson agreed. 'You've made a compelling case for me to have a very close look at how the investigation is being run. Thank you for bringing this to my attention. Anything you need, my door is always open, Ruth.'

Ruth nodded. 'Thank you, sir.'

Chapter 29

Ruth and Nick were waiting in a ground floor meeting room for Nina Taylor, who was a lawyer for the North Wales CPS. The Crown Prosecution Service – CPS – was the principal public body who was responsible for criminal prosecutions in England and Wales. They were headed by the Director of Public Prosecutions – the DPP.

The door opened and Nina came in. She was in her 30s, blonde, attractive, with a smart business suit and an expensive-looking briefcase. In her dealings with Nina, Ruth had always found her very approachable, but she clearly didn't suffer fools.

'Nina,' Ruth said in a friendly tone.

'Ruth,' Nina replied with a half-smile as she came and sat down at the meeting table.

'Have you met DS Nick Evans before?' Ruth asked.

'No, I haven't,' Nina replied, as she reached over and shook Nick's hand.

'Pleased to meet you,' he said.

They was a little look between them that Ruth noticed. She knew that some women found Nick attractive, and she'd had to keep an eye on him on a couple of occasions in the past. Not that she felt that he would ever cheat on Amanda. She would remove his testicles very slowly if he ever did. It's just that he could be a bit flirty and obviously liked the attention of attractive women.

'Likewise.' She smiled in Nick's direction. 'You guys aren't normally this side of the border,' she said.

Nick nodded. 'We've got an anomaly when it comes to the jurisdiction of Wayne Braddock's murder.'

'Yeah, I heard.' She gave him a knowing look. 'I've never heard of a body being found across the boundary line of two countries before.'

'Nope,' Nick agreed. 'Just when you thought you'd seen everything eh?'

'Indeed,' she said, still smiling at him.

He tilted his head and his eyes searched her face. 'Are you sure we haven't met before? You do look familiar.'

'No. I would have remembered if I'd met you before,' she answered, speaking softly.

Ruth saw Nick register the compliment and immediately try to hide his swollen ego.

Jesus! Yeah, let's get on with the business in hand please, Ruth thought to herself. *We might have a serial killer on our hands so less flirting.*

Ruth caught Nina's eye. 'We're pretty certain there's a link between Wayne Braddock's murder and the murder of Connor Barnard on Barmouth Beach last night.'

'Really?' Nina looked surprised. As she moved a tress of blonde hair from her face, Ruth saw a lovely delicate flower tattoo on her hand.

'And there was also an attempted murder over in Mold. Steve O'Connell?' Nick added.

Nina took a few seconds to process this and then said,

'Steve O'Connell? No one has ever been caught for the attack on him, have they?'

'No,' Ruth confirmed, 'but there is something that links all three attacks.'

Nina sat forward, looking intensely interested. 'What's that?'

'All the men had been charged with sexual assault and rape—' Ruth began.

'But the charges were dropped by the CPS,' Nina said, filling in the blanks as her eyes widened. 'I remember both the Steve O'Connell and Wayne Braddock cases. It broke my heart to have to tell the victims and their families that we just didn't have enough evidence to take those men to trial.' She narrowed her eyes. 'You really think that someone is targeting these men because they've had their rape charges dropped against them?'

Nick shrugged. 'It can't be a coincidence.'

'The MO on all the attacks has been the same,' Ruth explained. 'Blunt force trauma to the head with a hammer. Then stabbed with a screwdriver.'

'Have you got any witnesses to the attacks?' Nina asked.

Nick shook his head. 'Nothing.'

'But Steve O'Connell did hear the killer call out his name,' Ruth said. 'He seems to think that his attacker was a woman.'

'What?' Nina looked shocked. 'A woman? Really? Sorry, but I find that very difficult to believe.'

'He seemed pretty certain, and it's all we've got to go on,' Ruth added.

Nina paused in thought for a moment. 'How does this person know when the rape charges are dropped? It's not something that's in the public domain.'

'We thought you might be able to help us with that,' Nick explained.

'Could be a police officer,' she suggested.

'Yeah, we went down that route,' Ruth said dryly. 'It didn't go well.'

'We thought that you might be able to help us narrow down our search a little,' Nick said. 'There can't be that many people who would know about these cases.'

Ruth nodded. 'Something like a rape just doesn't get reported in the local press. And neither does it when charges for the offence are dropped. Which limits it to people who worked on those specific cases. We've looked at police officers, judges, and the legal teams and there's nothing to link them.'

Nina looked at them and pulled a face. 'To be honest, the court records are all online. They would record the preliminary hearing, the setting of bail, the intended trial date and then the CPS's decision to drop the charges.'

'And who has access to those records?' Ruth asked.

'Unfortunately, it could be anyone in the CPS offices, defence barristers and their staff, plus some of the administration team at the courts themselves,' Nina said, sounding almost apologetic. 'I'm really sorry guys, but it's not as small a pool of people as you might think.'

Ruth glanced over at Nick who gave her a frustrated look.

Chapter 30

As Ruth drained some pasta over the kitchen sink, she could feel the frustration of the day getting to her. The ongoing friction between her and DI Weaver was making her feel uncomfortable. And the conversation with Nina Taylor had left both her and Nick feeling a little flat. They had hoped that Nina would help them narrow down the investigation in terms of suspects. Plus, Ruth was anxious about hearing back from the adoption agency.

She was distracted and, as the pasta suddenly dropped into the colander, the steam rose up and scolded the side of her right hand.

'Shit!' she said, moving the colander over to the work surface. Then she went to run her hand under some cold water. 'Bollocks, bollocks.'

'You swear too much,' said a voice.

It was Daniel.

Ruth looked around and gave him an apologetic smile. 'Sorry, I burned my hand.'

Is it okay?' he asked.

'It'll be fine. It's my own silly fault.'

'You tell me not to swear,' he said with a shrug.

'Yeah, that's because you're eleven.'

'What age can I swear then?'

Ruth laughed. 'You can't.'

'What? Never?'

'No.'

Daniel looked confused. 'Some of the kids at school swear loads.'

'Do they?' Ruth asked, as she started to stir the bolognaise sauce on the hob.

'Katie Palmer told our PE teacher to 'fuck off' the other day,' he said, shaking his head. 'She's been suspended.'

'Good, but it's probably not a good idea to repeat exactly what she said.'

'Oh yeah,' Daniel said with a smile. 'Sorry.'

'Cheddar or Parmesan on your bolognaise?' she asked.

'Cheddar,' he replied, as though that was a silly question.

Then Ruth noticed that he was holding a piece of paper in his hand. 'What's that?'

'It's a permission slip. We're going on a school trip to the Imperial War Museum in Manchester and then we're going to the Arndale Centre.'

'Sounds great,' Ruth said, but something about Daniel's face suggested he was worried about going. 'Don't you want to go?'

'Yes,' he said hesitantly.

Ruth wasn't convinced. 'Are you worried about going to Manchester?'

'Sort of,' he admitted. 'It's just I've never been to a big shopping centre before. What if I get lost? Or what if the school bus goes without me?'

'They won't go without you,' Ruth said, trying to reassure him. 'You've got your phone if anything happens.'

He lowered his eyes and looked troubled. 'I wish you were going.'

'So do I,' she said with a smile. 'I tell you what. Why don't you put one of those tracker apps on your mobile phone. Then if you get lost or left behind, I can find you by looking at my phone.'

'No, it's all right,' he said, although she could see he was still worried. 'I might download it another time.'

Ruth smiled at Daniel's bravado. He didn't want to admit that he was scared.

He moved a little closer to Ruth. 'You know that lady?'

'What lady is that?' she asked, as she opened the cupboard to grab some plates.

'The lady that came yesterday to talk to me, you and Sarah.'

'Susannah?'

'Yeah. Has she told you anything about my adoption yet?'

Ruth could see that it was troubling him.

'No, not yet. But she'll be in touch very soon.'

'But what if they say you can't adopt me?' he asked, looking perturbed. 'Does that mean I can't live here anymore?'

'No,' Ruth said, shaking her head. She gave him a reassuring hug. 'It doesn't mean that at all.'

'Good,' he said, continuing to hug her, 'because I love living here.'

'And we love having you live here too,' she said.

Ruth didn't actually know what the effect of having an adoption application turned down by social services would have on their temporary foster care licence for Daniel. But it wasn't something she wanted to even think about at this stage.

Chapter 31

Georgie was drifting in and out of sleep as she lay on the sofa watching a nature programme on the television. She was dreaming about Jake. They were in a bar together, drinking, laughing and kissing. She felt so incredibly happy to be with him.

Her phone rang, jolting her awake.

She looked at the screen. It was Nick.

'Hi Nick,' she said, aware that her voice was a bit croaky.

'Hi,' he said. 'Did I wake you up?'

'Erm, yes, but it's fine,' she reassured him.

'I'm just checking you're okay and not sitting there fretting. But as you were fast asleep, I'm guessing not,' he said in an amused tone.

'I'm fine,' she laughed. 'Really. You don't have to keep checking up on me you know.'

'Actually, it was Amanda who made me ring,' he joked. 'I've seen you arrest a few very big scary men in the past, so I know you can handle yourself. In fact, you scare me sometimes.'

'Oh, shut up,' she chortled. Despite what she said, it was lovely to know that Nick and Amanda were on the end of the phone if she needed them.

'And the offer of staying here still stands,' he said.

'I'm fine, stop worrying,' Georgie insisted. 'You haven't told me how your meeting with Nina Taylor went. Isn't she the really attractive one from the CPS that you fancy?'

'No, I don't fancy her,' Nick laughed, 'and I'm sitting next to Amanda so thanks for that.'

Georgie giggled. 'Oh shit, sorry.'

'Yeah, I'm afraid Nina wasn't much help really. It was a bit frustrating. Anyway, as long as you're okay?'

'Yes, I am. Now sod off so I can go back to sleeping on the sofa,' she quipped.

'Right you are. I'll see you tomorrow,' he said, ending the call.

Georgie sat up and rubbed her face.

'Cup of tea and biscuits,' she muttered to herself as she stood up.

There was a loud knock at the door.

It startled her.

Her pulse quickened a little – she wasn't expecting anyone.

Trying to reassure herself that all the doors and windows were locked and secure, she went to the window in the living room and looked out at the porch and front door.

Nothing.

That's weird.

She was starting to feel uneasy. She hadn't ordered anything online for a while so it couldn't be a delivery.

This is ridiculous, she thought angrily as she marched into the kitchen, grabbed a knife, and went down the hallway to the front door.

She listened at it for a few seconds to see if she could hear any movement. Then she looked through the spyhole.

Nothing.

Gripping the knife, she opened the door and braced herself.

There was no one there and the cul-de-sac was deserted.

Looking down, she saw a small bunch of flowers that had been left on the doorstep. She reached down, picked them up, went back inside and locked the door.

Taking the flowers through to the kitchen, she put them down on the table and rummaged around for a card to say who they were from.

Except there wasn't a card.

Chapter 32

Pulling the car into a parking space at Chester Station, she checked her watch. It was 10.24pm. According to Rob Mills' social media, he was arriving back at Chester Station on the Birmingham train any minute now. Reaching onto the back seat, she took the black leather gloves and pulled them on. Then she reached under the passenger seat and took out a plastic bag. It gave a metallic clink as she opened it and then took out her trusty claw hammer and screwdriver which she had now cleaned thoroughly.

She pulled up the black hoodie over her head and placed the hammer and screwdriver into the inside pocket of her bomber jacket. Taking a deep breath, she tried to compose herself. It was clear that the police were getting closer to finding her. It wouldn't be long before she was caught but she didn't care. She wanted women everywhere to take the law into their own hands. And when she'd been caught, other women would take up her mantel.

Opening the door, she looked up to the sky. Despite the time, it was still an inky blue. The air was lovely and warm, and she got the faint smell of chips and fast food from somewhere. Normally it would have made her feel hungry, but she was too preoccupied with the task in hand.

Closing the car door, she wondered how many more summers she would see. She wondered where she might be next summer. Incarcerated somewhere perhaps? But by that time, she would be famous throughout the whole world. There were hardly any female serial killers, were there? There had been Myra Hindley and Rose West, but they had been psychotic bitches who had preyed on innocent children. What she was doing was a million miles from those evil women.

In fact the only person that she had found who had followed this path was the US serial killer, Aileen Wuornos. Between 1989-1990 she had worked as a prostitute and killed six clients who had either raped or attempted to rape her. Typically, she wasn't believed, and Wuornos was executed in Florida in 2002. It was a travesty and yet another example of society not allowing women to stand up for themselves or even protect themselves. In fact when she had watched the film 'Monster' about Aileen Wuornos, for which Charlize Theron won an Oscar for her portrayal, it had sewn a seed that had been whirling away in her mind for several years.

Looking up, she saw a stream of passengers walking out of the station, which signalled the arrival of a train. She narrowed her eyes, trying to spot her target. Rob Mills. Aged twenty-three. Arrested and charged with indecent assault and attempted rape of a sixteen-year-old girl, Rachel, over a year ago. And yet again, the system had let that poor girl down when the CPS were forced to drop the charges three weeks ago. It was another travesty, but she was about to get revenge for that innocent girl and her family. She'd sat with Rachel and her mother recently and had seen the damage and trauma that the attack had had on Rachel. Her mother described how her daughter had been a confident, outgoing and happy-go-lucky teenager before Robert Mills attacked her. Since then, she had been withdrawn, too nervous to travel anywhere on her own, and had started to self-harm as a way of trying to deal with the trauma.

Well, Robert Mills isn't going to get the chance to ruin anyone else's life, she thought, as she continued to scour the passengers coming out of the station.

Then she saw a young man wearing a black baseball cap walk out of the station. He had a phone to his ear, and he was chewing gum.

Bingo! she thought as she got a rush of adrenaline and her pulse quickened. She patted her jacket just to check that her weapons were there.

Mills jogged across the road, still talking and laughing to whoever he was on the phone with.

Yeah, well he won't be laughing for long, she thought as she turned and began to follow him up the road and into town.

Waiting for a bus and then two taxis to pass, she glanced across the road at The Town Crier pub where a group of drunken lads were shouting and laughing loudly. It startled her for a moment. She could feel them looking over at her.

Heading up City Road, Mills was about thirty yards ahead of her. Across the road, someone looked out of a first-floor window of the *Westminster Hotel*. She pulled her hood down over her face and quickly glanced the other way, hoping that no one had seen her.

Mills put his phone away in his pocket as he reached the bridge that straddled the canal. She watched as he took the shallow staircase that led down to The Old Harkers Arms and the towpath.

Shit!

For a few seconds, Mills was out of her sight, and she worried that she would lose him. He could go either way along the path or he could go into Harkers for a drink.

Breaking into a jog, she got to the stairs and to her relief she saw Mills walking away down Canal Side towards the *Artichoke*. She knew that in about five minutes the canal path would be far less busy and then she could strike.

She jogged a little more so that Mills was now only ten to fifteen yards ahead of her. Maybe he sensed her presence because he took a look back. It was far too dark for him to see her.

A few minutes later, the towpath was empty as they got to the part of Canal Side that was either industrial units or residential.

'Hey Rob,' she shouted.

Mills carried on walking and didn't look round.

That's weird. I know he heard me, she thought.

'Hey Rob,' she yelled again. 'Rob Mills.'

Mills stopped walking and turned to look at her.

'You talking to me?' he asked, looking confused.

'Yeah,' she said with a friendly smile. 'Rob Mills. Don't you remember me?'

He laughed. 'I think you've got the wrong person, love.'

Nice try, she thought as she pulled out the hammer and cracked it as hard as she could against his temple.

He crumpled to the floor with a loud groan.

All she could think about was poor Rachel and what this man had put her through.

Taking out the screwdriver, she swore that Rob Mills was never going to hurt a young woman ever again.

'What are you doing?' he protested, his face now covered in blood.

She drove the screwdriver into his Adam's apple. Pulling it out, she saw that his throat was totally exposed.

That'll do, she thought as she plunged the screwdriver into his chest and felt it hit a bone.

Chapter 33

It was early morning and Ruth had been summoned again to Superintendent Rickson's office. As she knocked on his door, she got that sinking feeling that she always seemed to get when faced with those in authority. Actually, it was men in authority. She seemed to handle women in authority with no problem. She had tried to get to the root of the problem but had found no answers. Sarah had once suggested that it was 'imposter syndrome' but it wasn't quite that. It was the feeling that she had done something wrong or that she was going to be caught out. It might have been some kind of deep-seated thing that she'd had with her father. That was the root of most problems, wasn't it? And her father had often been a tough man, difficult to please, with a quick temper. Maybe that was it.

'Come in,' said a voice.

Here we go, Ruth thought to herself. She assumed that it was going to be another development in her ongoing issue with DI Weaver. She was concerned that now he'd been backed into a corner, and possibly felt foolish, Weaver would retaliate like the petty little twat he was.

'Come in, come in,' Rickson said with a gesture.

Christ, he's being very friendly this morning, Ruth thought. Was that his way of smoothing over what going to be an uncomfortable conversation? She hoped not.

'Thank you, sir,' she said politely, as she lowered herself into the green padded chair and thought they could do with more comfortable chairs in the office they were occupying downstairs.

'Thank you for coming up so promptly,' Rickson said, as he gave her a serious look. 'I need to talk to you about something that's rather delicate.'

Oh God, now what? she wondered.

'Okay,' Ruth replied. 'Fire away, sir.'

'It's DI Weaver,' he explained.

Ruth's anxiety went up a notch. Weaver had thrown her under the bus and Rickson was going to ask the Llancastell CID team to step aside on the investigation.

'I'm afraid that DI Weaver has decided to take some time off,' Rickson said to clarify. 'He's been under a lot of stress recently and so we've come to a mutual agreement. He's going to take some time to recharge his batteries. And obviously the mental health and well-being of my officers is my priority.'

'Of course, sir,' Ruth said. This is not how she thought this conversation was going to go. 'The job can be very unforgiving sometimes.'

'Quite,' he agreed. 'So, now I have to ask you a favour.'

She gave him a quizzical look. 'Okay.'

He rested his elbows on the table and clasped his hands in front of him. 'I'd like you to take over from DI Weaver and lead the team on this investigation.'

'You mean the CID team here at Chester Town Hall?' Ruth asked. She wasn't sure how that was going to go down after the incident with Kelly Naylor.

'Don't worry, I've spoken to the troops. I assured them that you have my full backing,' Rickson explained. 'And if you get any resistance, my door is always open. I've spoken to Superintendent Clarke and he's more than happy for you to step in as SIO.'

'Right,' Ruth said, slightly taken aback by the request. However, it wasn't something she could exactly say no to. 'Of course, sir. I'll go down and get on with the morning briefing.'

She got up from her chair and gave him a polite nod.

'That's great,' Rickson said with a smile. 'Thank you, Ruth.'

Chapter 34

It was 9am as Ruth marched to the front of the CID office downstairs. Her pulse was racing and her mouth was dry. She hadn't felt this nervous since she took her first briefing at Llancastell CID. Back then, she had worried that the Welsh detectives wouldn't accept being led by a female officer who had just arrived from the London Met. She got that totally wrong, so she hoped that this briefing went to plan.

'Right everyone, listen up,' she said in her best authoritative tone. For a moment, the chatter continued, and she feared that they were just going to ignore her completely. She held her breath – but they quietened down, moved chairs, and turned to face her.

Over to the right were sat Nick, Garrow, French and Georgie. Nick gave her a reassuring wink.

Well, at least they're with me, she thought.

'Okay, as Superintendent Rickson explained, DI Weaver is taking some time away from work. So, until he returns, I've been asked to fill in and act as the SIO on this case.'

Ruth waited but there were no groans, mutters or whispers. It was a good sign.

'And I know that I didn't make myself very popular when Sergeant Kelly Naylor was questioned in connection to these murders,' she said, trying to sound as humble as she could, 'but in my defence, I didn't know Kelly and what an outstanding officer she is and how popular she is at this station.' Ruth held up her hands in a conciliatory gesture. 'My mistake, so I apologise for that.'

She noticed a couple of the detectives look at each other as if to say, 'Okay, she seems all right.'

Walking to the scene board, Ruth pointed to various photos. 'Okay, we have two murders and one attempted murder. All of our victims are single young men. And all of them have been charged with rape or sexual assault, only for the charges to be dropped. In fact, all three of these men were attacked within a few weeks of the CPS deciding not to take their cases to trial. We believe the killer is female, and she has used the same weapons for each of these crimes – a claw hammer and a screwdriver.' Ruth took a moment as she looked at the CID team who seemed to be taking her seriously. 'What we need to find out is what else, if anything, links these three men.'

DS Kennedy, whom Ruth had met at the crime scene the morning that Wayne Braddock's body had been discovered, looked up. 'What about a journalist?' she suggested.

'A journalist?' Ruth repeated, as she thought aloud.

'There are several journalists who work on the local newspapers and cover crime and the courts. They would be aware of the charges against the three men and that the scheduled trials hadn't gone ahead, and the charges then dropped.'

It was a good point, and something that she and her

team hadn't thought of. 'That's a good idea … sorry, I don't know your first name?'

'Jade,' Kennedy replied.

'Jade,' Ruth said, trying to make sure she remembered it. Now in her early 50s and perimenopausal, her memory was shockingly bad. 'Can you see what you can dig up for us, especially any female journalists?'

'Yes, ma'am.'

'Actually, 'boss' is just fine. I'm not a big fan of 'ma'am' as it makes me sound like I'm royalty or something.'

There were some smiles from the assembled detectives.

God, maybe they're even starting to like me!

Ruth spotted Nick wandering away to the side of the room to take a call on his mobile phone.

'I need us to trawl through all the victims' social media. Look to see if there are any links there. Friends, hobbies, places they go. That kind of thing.'

'Boss,' Nick called over with some sense of urgency.

'What is it?' she asked, with a growing sense of dread.

He looked uneasy. 'We've got another murder. And it's on the canal towpath again.'

Chapter 35

Twenty minutes later, Ruth and Nick pulled over and parked. They were closer to the centre of Chester than where they'd found Wayne Braddock's body. Getting out of the car, Ruth put on her sunglasses and then took out a packet of cigarettes.

'Wait a second,' she said, as she pulled out a ciggie and popped it into her mouth. 'I need one of these before I go and have a look.'

'Good job with the briefing,' Nick reassured her. 'They seem like a decent bunch.'

She lit her ciggie, took a deep breath and then blew out a long plume of smoke. 'Thanks,' she said with a smile. She knew that Nick had sensed her nervousness before taking the briefing.

'That's two murders in two days,' he said. 'Something has rattled our killer.'

'Looks like it,' Ruth agreed. 'Maybe she thinks that we're getting close to identifying her.'

'But we're not really, are we?'

'Thanks for your optimism,' Ruth said, as she took

another long drag. She didn't care what the doctors, Sarah, or anyone else said. Smoking was one of life's great luxuries and she could get hit by a bus tomorrow – so fuck 'em. 'Come on, we have narrowed it down a lot.'

'I just mean if our killer starts attacking people at this rate, we're going to need to move very fast.'

'Yeah, I know.' Ruth dropped her cigarette, stubbed it out with the heel of her shoe, and signalled for them to go.

'That's not very eco-friendly,' Nick joked as he pointed at the cigarette stub.

She pushed his arm playfully. 'Oh, shut up. It's bloody biodegradable, isn't it?'

He raised an eyebrow. 'Is it?'

Ruth ignored him as they walked from the car park to the canal towpath and turned right.

Up in front of them was a virtual carbon copy of the scene that had greeted them a few days ago when they'd arrived to see Wayne Braddock's body. Uniformed police officers in high-vis jackets, SOCOs in white forensic suits, and the white forensic tent over their latest victim's body.

'Jesus,' Nick muttered under his breath. 'Wait until the media get hold of the fact that we might have a female serial killer targeting young men. They're going to have a field day.'

'I know.' Ruth nodded in agreement. 'Rickson rang and asked me to do a press conference at twelve,' she said, looking at her watch.

Nick widened his eyes as they walked towards the police cordon. 'Christ, he really has thrown you in at the deep end.'

As they arrived at the police cordon, the female PC they'd seen only days earlier gave them a look of recognition. Before Ruth or Nick could pull out their warrant cards, she had lifted the police tape. 'It's okay ma'am, I remember you from last time.'

'Thank you, constable,' Nick said with a smile.

'Oi, I saw that,' Ruth said, raising her eyebrow.

'What?' Nick protested with a grin. 'I was just being friendly.'

'Yeah, well I spotted you getting 'friendly' with Nina Taylor from the CPS,' she said, giving him a disapproving look.

Nick shrugged. 'I can't help it if she finds me irresistible.'

Ruth shook her head and then wagged her finger. 'I can tell Amanda if you want me to.'

'Oh God, don't do that. She'd remove my balls and put them up on the wall.'

Before they could continue, DS Kennedy approached. She was already dressed in a white forensic suit.

'You beat us down here,' Ruth said, pointing to what she was wearing.

'I know a short cut,' she replied.

'What have we got?' Nick asked, as he gestured to the forensic tent.

'Identical. Same MO. Victim is a young male. Blunt force trauma to the head and multiple stab wounds.' She then held up a clear evidence bag which had something inside. 'But we have got his wallet. It was in his back pocket.'

Ruth peered at the bag. 'We know who he is then.'

'Yes, boss,' Kennedy replied as she looked at her notebook. 'Victim's name is Felix Monroe.'

'Address?' Nick asked.

'Yes,' Kennedy nodded and pointed down the towpath, away from the city centre, 'about a mile down there, boss.

I've organised a uniformed patrol to go round there and tell the next of kin.'

'Good work, Jade,' Ruth said. She was impressed by how quickly Kennedy had organised everything.

'First, we need find out whether or not Felix Monroe had any charges dropped against him recently,' Nick said, thinking out loud.

'I put a call in to Nina Taylor at the CPS,' Kennedy explained.

'Oh yes, we know Nina Taylor,' Ruth said, giving Nick a knowing look.

Kennedy sounded genuinely puzzled. 'That's the thing. Nina said the name didn't mean anything to her. She said she'd check, but she was pretty sure that Felix Monroe hadn't been charged with any crimes that she was aware of.'

That doesn't make any sense, Ruth thought.

Chapter 36

Ruth looked out at the press conference with some trepidation. Even though she'd held many press conferences over in Llancastell nick, this felt different. Plus, there were several national papers and broadcasters who were now picking up the story. And online, social media were already having a field day with their headlines and threads about another murder on the Chester canal towpath.

On the table in front of her was a jug of water and several small digital recorders and microphones that eager journalists had placed there. Sitting next to Ruth was Amit Popat, the Chief Corporate Communications Officer for Cheshire Police, who had come up from the main press office at Winsford. Popat was in his 30s, clean-shaven with black hair that was swept back off his face, and an affable manner.

'This is starting to get quite tricky,' he said under his breath as they looked out at the assembled journalists.

'At this stage, it's a question of damage limitation,' Ruth replied. 'And so far, we've had no eyewitnesses for any of the attacks. I'm hoping this will jog someone's memory.'

Popat nodded supportively. 'I'm doing my best to make sure this goes on the local TV news on both BBC and ITV.'

'That would be very useful,' Ruth said. It was a relief to have a press officer who wasn't a bloody know-it-all after her experiences with Kerry Mahoney, the rather snooty media officer for North Wales Police.

'Not that you need it, but good luck,' he said with a reassuring expression.

Ruth took a deep breath. *Come on, Ruth. You've done this dozens of times.*

'Good morning, everyone, I'm Detective Inspector Ruth Hunter and I am the senior investigating officer on what is a joint investigation between Cheshire Police and North Wales Police. I want to update you on developments in the last twenty-four hours as this is a fast-moving case. I can confirm that we're currently investigating three extremely violent murders that have taken place in the past few days. Two of those took place here in Chester, and one on the coast of North Wales at Barmouth.' Ruth turned and pointed to some enlarged photographs that had been positioned behind her. 'Wayne Braddock was murdered on the canal path that leads out of Chester city centre on Friday night between 11pm and 1am. Connor Barnard was murdered on the beach at Barmouth on Sunday evening between 6pm and 8pm. And Felix Monroe was also murdered on the Chester towpath last night between 11pm and 1am. These were horrific crimes against three defenceless young men. We are appealing for witnesses for all of these attacks, so we'd like to speak to any members of the public who were in those areas at those specific times, or saw any of the victims or anything suspicious.' Clearing her throat, Ruth continued. 'We are absolutely committed to finding whoever carried out these crimes. We are using every resource available to us to bring this investigation to a conclusion as quickly as possible. There are currently a number of lines of enquiry that we are exploring, but for obvious reasons I am unable to explain what those are. I do have a couple of minutes if there are any questions.'

Ruth braced herself as this was the most challenging part of any press conference as it required her to think on her feet.

A young female journalist at the front of the room indicated that she wanted to ask a question and Popat nodded in her direction.

'Emma Stevens, *Daily Express*,' she said. 'With two very violent attacks in Chester, can you reassure the city residents that they are safe to go about their lives in the usual way? Or are you advising people to stay away from the area where the attacks took place?'

'My advice would be for the residents of Chester and Barmouth to be as sensible and vigilant as they normally would be,' Ruth said, trying to remain as vague as she could, 'and to take the normal precautions when walking anywhere late at night.'

Popat pointed to a television journalist who was standing towards the back of the room. 'Vicky Newell, BBC News. Do you believe that you are looking for the same person for all of these three murders?'

'Yes, at this stage we do believe that the three murders are linked and that they were carried out by the same person.'

Newell raised an eyebrow. 'In that case, you are now looking for a serial killer, is that correct?'

Ruth knew that as soon as the phrase *serial killer* was banded about, with all the emotive, sensational and horrifying connotations, the national media would have a field day. And the population of Chester and North Wales would be thrown into panic.

'At this stage, I wouldn't like to comment on that,' Ruth said, hoping she could stall this line of questioning.

'Why not?' Newell asked.

Ruth ignored her but she could see some of the journalists were now talking and looking animated by what Newell had said.

Oh great. This is just what we need, she thought.

Ruth forced a tight smile as she answered Newell. 'I don't think that's a particularly helpful label. My focus is on trying to find out who is responsible for these attacks.'

Popat leaned forward to his microphone. 'Right, thanks everyone but that's all we've got time for.'

As Ruth and Popat got up, she gave him a grateful look for stepping in. 'Thank you.'

Chapter 37

Ruth was sitting in the DI's office that had been vacated by DI Weaver. It was poky, and darker than the one she had over at Llancastell where she at least had a window - even if the view over Llancastell wasn't exactly picturesque. Sitting back on the office chair, she took a deep breath.

'It's funny seeing you sitting there,' Georgie said, as she poked her head through the door. 'Do you think DI Weaver is okay?'

Ruth shrugged. 'No idea. I guess this job isn't great for your mental health at the best of times.' Then she gave Georgie an enquiring look. 'Everything all right at home?'

'No sign of any mystery stalker. But someone did leave a bunch of flowers on my doorstep, with no card.'

Ruth raised an eyebrow. 'That's a bit creepy.'

Georgie nodded. 'It is a bit, but I'm keeping vigilant.'

'You know I'm just a phone call away,' Ruth said, and then gestured to the printout that Georgie was holding in her hands. 'What's that?'

'I've searched the PNC and HOLMES for Felix Monroe,' she explained as she pulled a face.

'And?' Ruth asked with interest. The fact that the CPS hadn't heard of him had rung alarm bells earlier.

'Nothing, boss,' she said. 'Clean as a whistle. As they say in bad TV series, not even an unpaid parking ticket.'

Ruth tried to process the information. 'Bugger, that just doesn't make sense, does it?'

'Not really,' Georgie replied.

'I just can't think that there's anything else that links them,' Ruth said, thinking out loud. 'Anything else that might help us get a picture of Felix Monroe?'

Georgie looked down at her notes. 'He's twenty-seven, still lives at home with his mum in Upton. Works as a PE teacher, although according to the school he works at, Felix had been off work for a few months. The secretary I spoke to wasn't able to tell me why. She said that was something that would have been dealt with by Cheshire County HR.'

'Maybe he did attack someone, but he was just never arrested,' Ruth suggested.

Georgie clearly wasn't convinced. 'Maybe, but it doesn't really match the other attacks, does it?'

'No,' Ruth admitted. 'I'm just clutching at straws at the moment.'

'We've got a train ticket from his pocket,' Georgie said. 'Felix had been to Birmingham for the day. He arrived back at Chester Station at 10.26pm.'

Ruth went and looked at the large street map of Chester that was mounted on the wall. She pointed to a point on the canal. 'His body was found here. So if he was walking home, he would have walked up City Road and then taken Canal Side here. Let's get CCTV from anywhere along here. Also, there's a pub here …'

'Harkers,' Georgie said.

'Yes. Go and see if they have security cameras. And ask

if any of the staff saw anything suspicious around that time, or anyone acting strangely.'

'Yes, boss.'

'See if we can get CCTV from the station too,' Ruth added. 'I'd like to see Felix Monroe arriving and then follow his journey as much as we can from there.'

'Will do, boss,' Georgie replied. 'You've had a call from the mortuary over at the Chester Countess Hospital. They're doing a preliminary PM as we speak if you want to go over there.'

'Thanks Georgie,' Ruth said encouragingly. 'That's great work.'

Ruth walked out into the CID office and caught Nick's eye. 'We're going for a little drive.'

'Are we?' Nick asked.

'Yes,' Ruth replied. 'Thought you'd like to come with me to the preliminary PM.'

Nick gave her a wry smile. 'It's what I live for.'

Chapter 38

Ruth and Nick arrived at the double doors that led to the mortuary in the Countess Hospital. Everything seemed modern and clean compared to the University Hospital in Llancastell which dated back to the 19th century.

Pushing open the doors, Ruth was still wondering why Felix Monroe had been targeted the night before. What was the link?

A woman in her 50s, tall with red hair, dressed in pale blue scrubs, glanced over from the body that she was examining. She stopped what she was doing and walked towards them.

Ruth and Nick showed their warrant cards. It was the first time that either of them had been to this mortuary.

'Professor Barnes?' Ruth asked.

'Yes,' she replied in an uber confident, middle-class accent.

'DI Ruth Hunter and DS Nick Evans, Llancastell CID. I understand that you're expecting us?'

'Yes, yes,' Barnes said, as she pulled down her mask to

reveal a set of very expensive-looking teeth. 'Please, come over.'

Ruth approached the steel gurney and saw the white body of Felix Monroe laid out. As with the others, she could see the half a dozen or so stab marks to his chest, arms and neck.

'You must be acquainted with Professor Tony Amis?' Barnes said. 'Unless he's finally hung up his bloody scalpel.'

Barnes was a little too 'jolly hockey sticks' for Ruth's liking.

'No, Tony is still going,' Ruth said, as she gave Nick a wry smile.

'What can you tell us?' Nick asked, gesturing to the body.

'I've been through the notes on all the victims and this is identical. Blunt force trauma to the head, just here on the temple. Stab wounds that look the same.' She looked up at them and arched her brows. 'Of course, there is one major difference.'

Ruth pulled a face as she had no idea what that was.

Barnes pointed to the body. 'Felix Monroe was a transgender man.' She pointed to the chest area. 'You can see that there's some top surgery here.' She then pointed to his vagina. 'However, there hasn't been any phalloplasty surgery here. Obviously there's no way of knowing whether that was planned for the future. But this must strike you as strange?'

Ruth was still trying to process what she'd just learned about Felix Monroe. It just didn't add up, and it was definitely *strange* given the profile of the other victims.

'How do you mean?' Nick asked Barnes.

'The other victims were all young men who had been

accused of sexually assaulting young women,' Barnes said, 'and the charges against them had been dropped.'

Ruth got a sinking feeling. 'How do you know that?'

Barnes pointed to the mobile phone that was sitting on her desk. 'I've been reading about it online. It's all over social media, I'm afraid.'

Ruth looked at Nick. Just when she thought things couldn't get any worse.

Barnes then pointed to the body. 'I just can't see why this man was attacked.'

Ruth nodded in frustration. 'No, neither can I,' she agreed.

Chapter 39

Ruth had called an impromptu briefing of the CID team at Chester Town Hall nick. The investigation was moving fast, and she needed all the detectives to be up to speed.

'Right guys, listen up,' she said, as she walked over to the scene board which had now been updated with Felix Monroe's details and photograph. 'I know the developments in this case are moving fast, so I just need us to put our heads together before going any further.' She pointed to the photograph of Felix Monroe. 'Okay, this is Felix Monroe, our victim from last night. Aged twenty-seven, Felix was a PE teacher at a local school. He'd had some time off work recently but we're not sure why. DS Evans and I have just returned from the preliminary PM over at the Countess Hospital. The attack is identical to the other murders that we're investigating, so there is no doubt in my mind that Felix was murdered by the same person. However, there is one anomaly which doesn't fit our pattern. Not only does Felix Monroe have no criminal record at all, but he is also a transgender man.'

There were a few confused looks from the assembled

team. Felix just didn't fit the profile of the other victims at all.

'Up until now, we know our victims have been young men whose criminal charges for rape or sexual assault have been dropped,' Ruth said, and then raised an eyebrow. 'So, unless anyone has any ideas, I'm at a loss as to how Felix Monroe fits this pattern.'

DS French looked over. 'There must be something in Felix's life or background that made him a target.'

'But what is it?' Ruth asked.

There was a sea of blank expressions.

'Okay,' Ruth said, trying not to sound frustrated. 'Let's look at Felix's social media, phone records, bank records. Talk to the school he worked at. There has to be something that links him to the others.' Ruth headed across the room. 'If anyone needs me, I'll be in the office.' It was probably prudent not to refer to it as *her* office.

Ruth then had a thought. She spotted Nick, who was heading for the door, and called his name.

'Yes, boss?' he replied, stopping in his tracks.

'Change of plan. Let's go and talk to Felix Monroe's parents. See if they can shed any light on anything.'

'Right you are,' Nick said.

Chapter 40

Ruth and Nick had been at Felix Monroe's home for about ten minutes. Debbie Monroe, his mother, was clearly devastated as she sat on the sofa in their spacious living room. Using a tissue, she dabbed at her face where she'd been crying. She had informed them that her husband, Felix's father, had died a couple of years ago, so it was just the two of them now.

'I'm so sorry,' Debbie said, in her soft Scottish accent. 'I never offered you tea or coffee.'

Nick, who was writing in his notebook, gave her a kind smile. 'We're fine, thank you.'

'And did anything seem to be bothering Felix in recent weeks?' Ruth asked gently.

'No, nothing,' she replied. 'He's been so happy since he transitioned. It's made such a big difference to his life. Before that, he'd been so lost and unhappy.'

'Of course,' Nick said as he nodded.

Ruth leaned forward and looked at her. 'Can you think of anyone who wanted to harm Felix? Anyone that he'd fallen out with recently?'

'No,' Debbie said, but then she thought of something. 'Oh, there had been some silly stuff online since he'd transitioned. I think some of the kids at his previous school realised that he was the same teacher. But he seemed to take all that in his stride.'

Nick looked up from his notepad. 'And he'd never been in trouble with the police or been arrested?'

'God, no,' Debbie said, and her eyes filled with tears again. 'No. He was never any bother, even as a teenager … and now he's gone.' She tried to catch her breath.

Ruth gestured out to the hallway. 'Do you mind if we go and have a look in his bedroom?'

'Please,' Debbie sniffed. 'Take as long as you like. I want you to find out who did this to my son.'

'We're going to find out who did this to him, I promise you,' she reassured Debbie.

Ruth and Nick got up, went out to the tastefully decorated hallway and then went up the stairs.

The wall up the stairs was adorned with family photos.

At the top of the stairs, Nick went to the nearest door and looked back at Ruth. 'This looks like it.'

They walked into the tidy bedroom. There were some fairy lights hung across the white iron bedstead. Over to the left, there was a large television and a turntable with some vinyl albums next to it.

Nick went over to the wardrobe and began to look through it. Ruth went over to a desk where there was a laptop. Then she crouched down and looked under the bed.

Nothing.

After a few minutes, Ruth decided to call it quits. Nothing that Debbie Monroe had told them, or their search of Felix's bedroom, had provided any clues as to why he'd been targeted the previous night.

It was incredibly frustrating.

Chapter 41

Ruth and Nick walked along the corridor towards the CID office. They were still perturbed that they seemed to be no closer to finding a viable suspect for the murders. And after their trip to see Debbie Monroe, Ruth was more confused than ever. She feared that if they didn't find a suspect soon, there would be another murder.

Pushing open the double doors to the office, there was a palpable sense that something was up. Several officers were crowded around a computer at the far end.

Garrow spotted them coming in and approached. 'We think we've found something, boss,' he said, giving her a meaningful look.

Ruth could see that whatever it was, it seemed significant enough for her to feel a little more positive.

Georgie looked over from the huddle of detectives and then pointed to the monitor that was mounted up on the wall. 'There's something you need to see, boss.'

'Okay,' Ruth said, exchanging a look with Nick as if to say, 'What's going on?'

The monitor on the wall burst into life and Ruth could

see CCTV footage. It looked like the entrance and car park for Chester Station.

Georgie came over and stood next to Ruth. 'This is the CCTV from last night.'

The timecode at the bottom of the screen read *10.26pm*.

As the CCTV played, Ruth could see a stream of passengers exiting Chester Station and heading in all directions to get taxis or meet those that were there to pick them up.

Georgie went closer to the screen and pointed to a figure wearing a baseball cap and talking on a mobile phone as he left the station. 'Right, that's Felix Monroe arriving back from Birmingham.'

Peering closely, Ruth watched carefully as Felix crossed the road beside the station and then headed up City Road towards the city centre as she had predicted.

Ruth gave Georgie a questioning look. What she had shown her didn't seem particularly significant.

'Okay,' Georgie said, as the CCTV played backwards.

Ruth wondered what she was meant to be looking at now.

'Now watch this person here.' Georgie pointed to a figure with a black hoodie over their head. As the CCTV played again, it was clear that this person was watching Felix as he came out of the station. And then, as he passed them, the hooded figure began to follow him up the road into town.

Jesus, that must be our killer, Ruth thought as a chill ran up her spine.

Ruth went close to the screen and peered at the image, but it was hard to deduce anything about the figure that was following Felix.

'Okay, can we pick them both up as they get further up City Road?' she asked, feeling her pulse quicken.

Georgie shook her head. 'We're still waiting for the council to get the CCTV over to us.'

Then Ruth had a thought. She looked over to where the detectives were gathered.

'Where does this person come from?' Ruth asked, as she pointed again at the screen. 'Can we see what direction they arrive from? Play it back to about *10.20pm* please.'

The CCTV footage was played back to *10.20pm*, but because of the image quality as it rewound, it wasn't possible to see where or when the figure had appeared in that area.

'Just play it from here,' Ruth called over, sounding a little impatient.

The CCTV of the station entrance and car park played again. It was now virtually empty.

Ruth went closer to the screen, scrutinising every movement, every car, taxi or pedestrian that appeared anywhere.

Over in the car park, she saw the door to a red Mini Clubman open. Someone got out but it was too far away to see any details.

However, as that person closed the driver's door, they then pulled a black hoodie up and over their head.

'There!' Ruth pointed forcefully at the screen. 'This person here.'

As the CCTV played forward, the hooded figure walked slowly towards the pavement and waited.

And then, as Ruth had seen before, the hooded figure watched and followed Felix Monroe.

'I need the number plate of that Mini,' Ruth said urgently, still transfixed by what she was looking at. 'Can you zoom in any tighter?'

A few seconds later, the screen flickered and then jumped as the image magnified.

Adjusting her eyes, Ruth could now read the plate.

'I need an urgent DVLA check on a Lima Delta Zero Nine, Yankee Foxtrot Alpha,' she said loudly.

She spotted that Nick had already jumped onto a computer and was typing furiously at the keyboard. 'I'm on it,' he reassured her.

Ruth held her breath. If this really was their killer, then the registration might give them a name and address.

Unless it's a false plate, she thought pessimistically.

After a few seconds, Nick stopped and turned around.

His eyes widened as he gave her a dark look.

'What?' Ruth asked, wondering what on earth he'd discovered.

'That Mini belongs to Nina Taylor,' he said.

Chapter 42

Walking along the top corridor, Ruth was making her way towards Superintendent Rickson's office, feeling dumbfounded by what they had just discovered. If they really did believe that a top crown prosecution lawyer was responsible for the murders, she needed to let him know. It was politically very sensitive, and she wanted to run it past him before acting on the evidence.

Knocking on Rickson's door, she heard the customary 'Come in' and entered.

'Hi Ruth,' he said politely as he gestured to a seat. 'Come and sit down.'

'Thank you, sir,' she said as she came over.

'I'm glad you're here,' he said, and then he pointed to his mobile phone that was sitting on the desk. 'As you've probably seen, we're taking a bit of a hammering on social media. I've had the chief constable on the phone this morning asking me when he can expect to see progress, a suspect, or an arrest. I did tell him how complex it was to buy us some time.'

Ruth looked at him uneasily. 'Well, sir, we do have a significant development, but it's not entirely good news.'

Rickson gave her a quizzical look. 'Explain?'

'We found CCTV footage of a person outside Chester Station from last night. That person waited for and then followed Felix Monroe, the young man who was murdered on the towpath last night.'

Rickson sat forward with this news. 'Any way of identifying that person?' he asked hopefully. Ruth knew that the pressure was on Rickson to deliver at least a prime suspect as quickly as possible.

'CCTV shows that person getting out of a car. It's a Mini Clubman that was parked at Chester Station. The same person returns to that car 45 minutes later,' Ruth explained. 'I'm convinced it's our killer.'

'So, what's the problem?' Rickson asked.

She gave him a meaningful look. 'That car belongs to Nina Taylor, a senior lawyer at the Crown Prosecution Service in North Wales.'

Rickson narrowed his eyes in disbelief. 'What?'

'I know that it's very positive news that we have a suspect,' Ruth said. 'But I've worked with Nina Taylor in the past few years and I'm in complete shock that she might be responsible for these murders.'

'It doesn't make much sense,' Rickson agreed, 'but you can't actually identify her from the CCTV?'

'No, sir,' Ruth replied. 'Of course, we can't confirm that it's her using that car until we bring her in for questioning. It could be someone else.'

'I understand but—' Rickson said.

There was a loud knock at the door.

'I'm not expecting anyone.' He frowned and then boomed, 'Come in.'

The door opened and Nick poked his head in.

'I'm so sorry to interrupt, sir,' he said, 'but I have something that I need to show both you and DI Hunter urgently.'

Rickson gestured. 'Come in.'

As Nick walked across Rickson's office, Ruth saw that he was carrying a small laptop under his arm. He sat down, opened the laptop, and waited for the screen to come to life.

'We have checked the CCTV throughout the city centre from last night, but we couldn't find any more sightings of the person that we saw following Felix Monroe.' He then clicked a button on the laptop. 'However, a woman was standing outside Harkers pub last night taking videos of her friends on her iPhone. When she saw what she'd filmed and then saw the news, she called us and sent us this video.'

Ruth leaned forward and peered at the screen as Nick played the wobbly footage. There was a drunk woman in her 50s in the frame, laughing and pointing. Behind her was the canal towpath, the bridge over the canal, and the staircase that led up to City Road.

A figure appeared coming down the stairs. As they headed towards where the person with the iPhone was standing, Nick paused the video and pointed.

'So, this is Felix Monroe, sir,' he said, showing Rickson.

'Okay,' Rickson said, completely absorbed in what Nick was showing him.

Nick pressed play again and the video continued. Felix Monroe walked past the camera and out of shot.

Behind, Ruth could see someone else coming down the stairs. As they approached, she could see it was someone wearing a bomber jacket with a black hoodie up over their head. They were walking very quickly.

As they got close to the camera, Nick paused the video again.

Ruth looked at the face that peered out from under the hoodie.

Her stomach tightened. It was a face that she recognised.

'And this is Nina Taylor,' Nick said, as he pointed at the image.

Their fears were confirmed.

Rickson gave them a sombre look. 'You'd better bring her in.'

Chapter 43

Ruth and Nick pulled into the car park at Mold Crown Court. They were still stunned by what they had seen on the CCTV and the terrible thought that Nina Taylor could be responsible for the string of violent murders.

They pulled into a car parking space and got out. A uniformed patrol pulled into the space next to them.

'Over there,' Nick said, as he pointed to the red Mini Clubman that they'd seen on the CCTV that belonged to Nina Taylor.

They had confirmed that Nina was in court today. Ruth wanted to check the vehicle and then get it taken away for forensics before they arrested Nina. She had also organised an arrest warrant which was in her pocket in case Nina tried to resist coming with them on a legal technicality. She was a lawyer after all.

Ruth signalled to the two uniformed officers to follow her over to the Mini. 'We're over here, guys.'

They all made their way towards the car. The older of the uniformed officers – 50s, bald, glasses – pulled on blue forensic gloves. Then he took a small, specialised hammer and went to the driver's window. He began to tap hard at the glass until it broke. He used the hammer and his hand to pull the glass out of the window, then reached in and opened the door from the inside.

Nick approached, pulling on his blue forensic gloves as he went. He sat on the driver's seat and began to carefully look around the car.

Ruth came around and peered inside. 'Anything?'

'Nothing yet,' he said, but then he put his hand under the passenger seat and pulled out a white plastic bag. It gave a metallic clink as he lifted it up. Opening it, he gave a dejected sigh.

Ruth frowned as he passed the bag for her to look inside.

A screwdriver and a claw hammer.

Chapter 44

Ruth and Nick marched into Mold Crown Court and headed straight for the reception desk.

Ruth's phone rang and she answered it.

'DI Hunter,' she said.

'Boss?' It was Georgie.

'Hi Georgie,' Ruth said. 'Can I call you back?'

'I've got something that I thought you'd want to know straight away,' she explained.

'Okay,' Ruth said, now wondering what Georgie had discovered.

'I checked everyone who booked a ticket on the train from Birmingham that Felix Monroe was on last night,' she said. 'Then I ran those names through the PNC, and we've got a hit.'

'Go on.'

'There was a Robert Mills on the same train as Felix, and Robert Mills is 24 years old. He was arrested and charged with indecent assault and the attempted rape of a sixteen-year-old girl, Rachel Bentley, over a year ago. The CPS were forced to drop the charges three weeks ago.'

'Bloody hell,' Ruth said under her breath. 'Felix Monroe was murdered because Nina Taylor mistook him for Robert Mills.'

'It looks that way, boss,' Georgie replied.

'Tell the others that we found the murder weapons in Nina Taylor's vehicle,' Ruth said quietly. 'We're going to arrest her and bring her in.'

'I'll let everyone know,' Georgie said. 'And I know it's not exactly the result we wanted, but it's still a result.'

'I know,' Ruth said. 'See you later.'

Ruth flashed her warrant card. 'Can you tell me where Nina Taylor from the CPS is today?'

The receptionist – female, 30s, brunette – gave her a polite smile. 'I'll just check for you.' She then went to a computer and typed for a couple of seconds. 'She's in Court No 3 today.'

'Thanks,' Nick said.

Ruth and Nick marched up the steps to the main corridor and headed for the entrance to Court No 3.

There was a burly-looking security guard outside. 'Can I help?'

They both flashed their warrant cards.

He nodded and opened the door for them. 'There is a trial currently in progress,' he said under his breath, as a way of telling them to keep noise to a minimum.

Ruth soon spotted Nina Taylor sitting on her own on a bench behind the prosecution barristers and their team. In the far corner of the court, a witness was being questioned by a defence barrister with a booming voice. Nina was absorbed in watching the witness and didn't notice their arrival.

'She's over there,' Ruth whispered to Nick as she made a subtle gesture in Nina's direction.

Ruth and Nick split up just in case Nina tried to do a

runner. Arriving at the end of the bench, Ruth looked along and caught Nina's eye for a second.

She gave Ruth a curious look before turning and spotting that Nick was coming down the bench towards her.

Her face fell – she knew something was up.

Ruth moved along the bench and sat down next to her just as Nick reached the other side and did the same.

'I'm going to need you to come with me please, Nina,' Ruth whispered.

Nina looked straight ahead as if Ruth hadn't said anything.

Ruth touched her arm to get her attention. 'Nina?'

'Don't touch me,' she hissed, as she shrugged off Ruth's hand aggressively.

'Nina?' Nick whispered.

For a few seconds, Nina didn't respond. Then she slowly turned to look directly at Ruth. She had an icy stare.

'What do you want?' she asked in an angry whisper.

Ruth met her stare. 'We know, Nina. I'm going to need you to come with us back to Chester Town Hall Police Station please. I do have an arrest warrant here if you'd like to see it.'

Nina took a few seconds and gave them both a sarcastic smile.

Then she stood up very slowly. 'We'd better get going then.'

Chapter 45

'Interview conducted with Nina Taylor, 1.30pm, Chester Town Hall Police Station. Present are Nina Taylor, Detective Sergeant Nick Evans, Duty Solicitor Shirley Williams, and myself, Detective Inspector Ruth Hunter.'

Nina was now dressed in a grey sweatshirt and bottoms. Her clothes had been taken for extensive DNA analysis. Her mouth had been swabbed for a DNA sample and her nails clipped.

Having secured a search warrant, Nina's property was now being searched by the forensic team. Her phone and bank records had also been requested.

Nina gave Ruth an icy stare and then leaned in to talk to Williams and whispered something in her ear.

Ruth raised her eyebrow. 'Nina, do you understand that you are still under arrest for murder?'

Nina's eyes were quick and sharp, and she peered over at Nick with the faintest hint of a smirk. 'No comment.'

Are you kidding me? Ruth thought with frustration.

Nick shifted forward in his seat. 'Nina, I'd like to advise you that opting for a "no comment" interview isn't in your

180

best interests here. The evidence against you is over-whelming and so some explanation is going to be needed.'

As a CPS lawyer, Nina was more than aware of the right and wrong way of approaching a police interview, so it was frustrating that she'd chosen to go down this route.

Nina sat back, gently moved a strand of hair from her face, and then gave Ruth a bemused shrug. 'No comment.'

Ruth couldn't believe the woman sitting in front of her was the same person that she had dealt with from the CPS in the past few years. She had completely transformed in terms of her body language, the way she held herself, and the look on her face. It was hard to pinpoint what was so different, as on the surface Nina obviously looked the same. But there was something so different that it was chilling to witness. In fact Ruth felt a chill shiver up her spine as she glanced over at her.

Nick reached across the desk, pulled over a laptop, and opened it. He then tapped a few buttons. 'For the purposes of the tape, I'm showing the suspect Item Reference 398G.' He turned the laptop so Nina could see. 'This is CCTV footage from outside Chester Station last night. We believe that this person standing here is you. Is there anything you'd like to tell us about that?'

She gave Nick a withering look. 'No comment.'

He pointed to the screen. 'And this young man here is Felix Monroe who was brutally murdered on the canal towpath last night. Is there anything you can tell us about that?'

'No comment.'

'As you can see,' Nick continued, 'this person here waits for Felix, and as he passes they follow him up City Road into Chester city centre. However, if we play this CCTV back a bit, you can see that this person gets out of this red Mini Clubman four minutes before Felix leaves the station.

The registration of that vehicle is LD09 YFA. Does that registration mean anything to you?'

Nina shook her head and looked at the floor.

'For the purposes of the tape, the suspect has indicated that the registration LD09 YFA doesn't mean anything to them.'

Nick leaned forward and stared at her. 'Would it surprise you to know that the vehicle, this red Mini Clubman, is registered to you at your home address. Is there anything you can tell us about that, Nina?'

Nina gave a withering groan, and without looking up replied, 'No comment.'

Ruth turned to Nick with a bewildered look on her face. Whoever was sitting in that seat, she seemed to bear no resemblance to the woman Ruth had known to be a sharp, businesslike, CPS lawyer.

Nick then pressed another button on the laptop. 'For the purposes of the tape, I am now going to show the suspect Item Reference 783B.' He moved the laptop back for Nina to look at.

She was still staring at the floor.

'Nina, could you look at this video for me please?' he asked.

'No,' she mumbled.

Nick clicked the spacebar and the video from the iPhone played. 'Nina, this is a video that was taken outside the Harkers pub last night. Here we can see our victim Felix Monroe walking past the camera. And then this here …' he paused the video so that Nina's face was now in the middle of the screen, 'this is you, isn't it, Nina?'

Nina looked up and then peered over at the laptop. 'No comment.'

'Can you tell us what you were doing last night, walking past Harkers along the canal towpath?' he asked.

Nina raised her eyebrows and glared at him. 'No comment.'

Ruth waited for a few seconds to allow the tension in the room to build a little. Then she leaned forward and looked directly at Nina.

'You weren't waiting for Felix Monroe last night, were you, Nina?' she asked.

Nina didn't answer.

'In fact, you were waiting for another young man. Robert Mills,' Ruth continued. 'Robert Mills was arrested and charged with the indecent assault and the attempted rape of a sixteen-year-old girl in Chester a year ago, wasn't he? But three weeks ago, the charges against him were dropped. As a CPS lawyer, you must have been gutted when you learned that. The same as Steve O'Connell, Wayne Braddock and Connor Barnard. All young men who had been arrested and charged with rape or sexual assault. And all young men who you thought had got away with it. But you felt that wasn't fair on the victims. In fact it made you very angry, especially those victims who you had spent a lot of time with. You'd seen the kind of emotional and psychological damage that kind of traumatic event can have on a young woman. They're never the same again. They have to try and rebuild their lives. And the one thing that might help them do that is knowing that the man who attacked them had been punished for what they had done.'

There were a few seconds of silence.

Nina just glared at Ruth.

'I understand that, Nina. I'm a police officer. I've seen men like that walk free for years. And it makes me sick,' Ruth said. 'But you decided to take the law into your own hands and dish out your own form of justice on them, didn't you?'

Nina didn't respond.

'Except with Felix Monroe you made a huge mistake, because you mistook him for Robert Mills. And you followed him from the station and murdered him. An innocent young man who hadn't harmed anyone.'

Nina had a defiant expression on her face. 'Yeah, I did.'

'Sorry?' Ruth said, shocked that Nina seemed to have suddenly made a confession.

'I did kill him. I killed them all because that's what they deserved,' she said in a nonchalant tone. 'You're a woman. You know what it's like out there. The world is a better, safer place without them. You can't argue against that, Ruth.'

Ruth took a moment. 'What about Felix Monroe?'

'He was probably the same,' Nina said. 'I saw him yesterday coming out of the station. Full of himself. It was only a matter of time before he'd hurt a woman. It was inevitable.'

'Except it wasn't,' Ruth said, shaking her head, 'because Felix was a transgender man.'

Nina's eyes widened as her face fell. 'What?'

'If there was anyone on the planet who was likely to treat women with respect, it was Felix Monroe,' Ruth said sadly. 'And you killed him.'

Nina's expression turned quickly into one of shock – she was lost for words.

Chapter 46

Ruth and Nick had followed the blacked-out prison van that was transporting Nina to her plea hearing. Given the severity of her crimes, and the growing media storm surrounding her arrest, there had been two uniformed patrol cars and four police motorcycles. There had also been a media scrum of photographers, reporters and television crews when Ruth and Nick had made their way into Chester Crown Court.

Sitting in the public gallery, Ruth looked over at Nina, who was now dressed in a smart business suit and sitting next to a female prison officer. She had the same cold, vacant look that she'd had when they'd questioned her earlier.

The judge was a grey-haired man in his seventies, wearing thick rimmed glasses and a stern expression. He glanced at Nina. 'Will the defendant please rise.'

Nina and the female prison officer stood.

'Miss Taylor, you are here this afternoon to enter a plea for the crimes with which you have been charged. Do you understand that?' he asked.

'Yes, your honour,' Nina replied in a calm, clear voice.

'Can you confirm that you are Nina Lucy Taylor?'

'Yes, I can confirm that,' she said.

'Miss Taylor, you are charged with four counts of murder contrary to common law. How do you plead to these charges?' he asked her.

'Guilty, your honour.'

There were a few gasps from the relatives in the public gallery.

'Thank God,' Nick whispered to Ruth.

She nodded. She was relieved that they didn't now have to prepare for a criminal trial, with all the work that would entail. It also spared the victims' relatives months of anguish in the lead-up to the trial, as they feared that Nina might not be convicted.

'You may sit down, Miss Taylor,' the judge said, as he peered at some paperwork in front of him.

'Actually,' Nina said loudly, 'I'd like to use this opportunity to tell everyone that my crimes were committed because of the failure of courts like this and the judicial system to punish men who attack, assault, and rape innocent women. Men who go unpunished.'

'Silence, Miss Taylor,' the judge snapped, 'or I'll hold you in contempt of this court.'

'I'm not worried about that your honour,' Nina snorted. 'I'm about to spend the rest of my life in prison. This country is facing an epidemic of these sorts of crimes. Eight million women over the age of sixteen have experienced some form of sexual assault. And nearly two million of them have been raped. Their lives have been ruined by men, 98% of whom are never convicted.'

The judge glared at the female prison officer who was attempting to stop Nina from talking. 'Silence in court. Take her down please, officer.'

'It's time that women took back the streets of this country and showed men that they're no longer willing to be victims of these crimes,' she shouted, as the prison officer tried to pull her away and get her out of the court.

'I will adjourn sentencing until the defendant can behave herself in a manner that is appropriate for this courtroom,' the judge boomed loudly. 'She will be remanded in custody until then,' he said, looking increasingly angry.

The female police officer had now been joined by two burly court security guards who were dragging Nina towards the exit.

'I urge all women to take the law into their own hands until the judicial system can adequately protect us!' she yelled.

Ruth's eyes widened as she looked at Nick. She hadn't seen anything quite like this in all her time as a police officer.

The judge glared over at Nina. 'Miss Taylor, I can tell you now that the sentence will be imprisonment for life. The only issue will be the minimum term I must impose pursuant to Sentencing Act 2020. And whether you like it or not, I will be charging you with contempt of this courtroom.'

The security guards and the female prison officer managed to get Nina out of the exit that led down to a security area. From there she would be taken by prison transporter to HMP Tonsgrove, a female prison over on Anglesey.

'Come on, we'd better get down there,' Ruth said as she stood up. Nina was still their prisoner until she arrived at Tonsgrove, and Ruth wanted to make sure that she got on that transporter without a hitch.

As they moved swiftly along the seats and headed out

of the public gallery, Ruth saw Debbie Monroe approaching.

'DI Hunter,' she said, still looking upset by what she'd witnessed in court. 'I just wanted to thank you for catching the person who took Felix from me.'

'Of course,' Ruth said with a kind smile. She pulled out her contact card which she handed to her. 'And if there's anything you need going forward, please don't hesitate to get in touch with me.'

Debbie looked at the card. 'That's very kind of you. Thank you.'

Ruth and Nick hurried out of the public gallery, along the corridor, and over to the door at the rear of the court-house that led towards the holding area.

They flashed their warrant cards to the security guard on the door and he opened it for them.

'Jesus,' Nick said, blowing his cheeks out as they came down the back staircase. 'That was bloody chaotic.'

'Yeah, I've seen defendants lose their temper before,' Ruth said, 'but nothing like that.'

Coming to the double doors, Nick pushed them open, and they came out to the outside holding area.

Nina was standing to one side flanked by two prison officers. Both her hands were cuffed in front of her in preparation for her journey to HMP Tonsgrove.

The huge steel doors slid open noisily and the white prison transporter pulled in very slowly and then stopped.

The prison officer driving it – male, 50s, skinny – jumped out and looked at them.

'Right, I'm running late so let's get on with it,' he said in a thick Scouse accent.

The two female prison officers put their hands on Nina's shoulders as they directed her towards the rear door of the transporter.

Suddenly there were shouts from above.

'Nina? Nina? Up here,' yelled the voices.

Everyone stopped to look up.

Ruth saw a huddle of press photographers standing on the low roof of a garage, trying to take photos of Nina.

'This way, Nina! Over here!' one of them shouted.

'For fuck's sake,' Nick growled.

Ruth and Nick moved towards the roof.

'Oi, get down from there!' Nick shouted angrily as he gestured at them.

Ruth got out her warrant card and pointed to the photographers. 'I want you lot off of there, or I'm arresting you for breach of the peace.'

As they backed away, one of them stumbled forward, lost his footing, and fell from the roof onto the concrete below. He landed on his head and then his back with a crunch.

'Oh shit!' Ruth yelled, as she and Nick sprinted over.

The photographer lay in a heap, unconscious on the ground, his face covered in blood.

Nick looked at Ruth with concern in his eyes. 'This is not good.'

She pulled her radio from her belt and pressed the button. 'Three six to control,' she said urgently, 'are you receiving me, over?'

'Control to three six, we are receiving you,' said the computer aided dispatch operator. 'Go ahead, over.'

Nick crouched down and examined the photographer.

'I need paramedics as quickly as possible to the rear entrance of Mold Crown Court,' Ruth said. 'I have an unconscious male who has fallen and has a serious head injury, over.'

'Received, three six,' the CAD said. 'Stand by, I will advise, over.'

The three prison officers came over to see if they could help.

The first officer to reach them - a woman in her 40s with short, black, cropped hair - crouched down by the photographer and began to feel for his pulse.

'I'm a senior first aider at the prison,' she told Ruth as she leaned over the injured man. 'Yeah, he's not breathing so I'm going to have to perform CPR.'

Ruth and Nick moved back a couple of paces to allow her more space.

She crouched over his head and looked up at Ruth. 'I'm going to need you to pump his chest in a regular rhythm in between me breathing into his mouth. Okay?'

Ruth nodded. She had seen CPR administered on several occasions, but she had never performed it.

The officer tilted the photographer's head back so that his windpipe was horizontal, then she pinched his nostrils and breathed into his mouth. Then she looked to Ruth, who started to pump his chest with two hands to the rhythm of the Bee Gees' *Staying Alive* which she'd seen on the television.

'Okay, and stop,' the officer said, holding up her hand as she went back to breathing into his mouth. Then she stopped and looked at Ruth. 'And again.'

Ruth continued with the chest compressions.

'Okay, he's breathing,' the officer said finally in a relieved tone.

Taking a breath herself, Ruth stood up with a huge sense of relief that the man's chest was now slowly rising and falling.

'Jesus,' the officer said, blowing out her cheeks as she stood.

Looking up, Ruth could see the other photographers looking down in concern.

'Good job,' Nick said to Ruth and the prison officer.

'Thanks.' She turned to look at Nick, but her eyes were drawn to the secure yard behind.

It was empty.

'Where the hell is Nina?' Ruth said, as she froze.

Nick spun around. 'What?'

Everyone turned in panic as they scoured the holding area.

'Oh, you have got to be joking!' Ruth growled. She broke into a sprint, went past the prison transporter and through the steel doors that opened on to the road.

Looking left and then right, Ruth saw that the road was deserted.

Nick ran over to her, his eyes wide with concern.

Nina Taylor had escaped.

Chapter 47

Ruth looked out from the DI's at the CID office which was now a hive of nervous energy. They had a killer on the loose who was desperate and very dangerous. Ruth was angry with herself for taking her eyes off Nina at the courthouse and allowing her to escape. Having just taken over as SIO on the investigation, and with a whole new CID team under her leadership, this was an utter disaster. She wondered if Rickson would take her off the case.

Putting that thought to one side, Ruth began to run through all the possible scenarios. The major roads out of the city now had police checks on all vehicles. There were also officers at the train and coach stations. However, Nina could also be hiding out somewhere in the city and biding her time. She could even be in someone's home, holding them hostage until things calmed down a bit. That scenario didn't bear thinking about.

Ruth's phone vibrated and she looked down to see a BBC News headline – *Killer is now on the run following her escape from court.* The major UK newspapers, television and radio were now covering what had happened and most had it as their lead story. And social media was a frenzy of people – and so-called experts – demanding to know how Nina Taylor had managed to escape while in custody. The fact that a claw hammer and screwdriver had been used to murder the three young men – Felix Monroe, Connor Barnard and Wayne Braddock – had been picked up by several online versions of tabloid newspapers. And so the obvious comparisons to Peter Sutcliffe had been made. And now the term *The Towpath Ripper* was being bandied around, much to Ruth's horror.

She walked slowly over to a series of scene boards that stood at the far end of the office. She knew that she couldn't dwell on Nina's escape and who was at fault. After all, a photographer had died for a few minutes in front of her eyes and she had helped to save his life.

Scouring the scene boards, she saw that they were covered in writing, photographs, maps and other pieces of evidence. Red pins on a map of Chester and North Wales showed where the men had been attacked.

The photograph of Felix Monroe was pinned to the left-hand side. His bright, smiling face beamed out of the dark strands of hair that curled on his forehead. His deep blue eyes had a twinkle in them, as if he'd just heard a joke.

Felix Alistair Monroe. Born May 23rd 1994.

Ruth studied the image for a few seconds. So full of life. So blissfully unaware of the horrific, devastating and untimely way it would end. It was a terrible tragedy.

Then her eyes were drawn to the other two photos – Wayne Braddock and Connor Barnard. Her feelings about them were a little more ambivalent. She didn't accept what Nina Taylor maintained. That these men had ruined the lives of young women and therefore deserved to die. If they were proved guilty in a court of law, then Ruth was

SIMON MCCLEAVE

happy for them to feel the full force of the law, and for the women and their families to get justice for what had happened to them. Ruth had never believed in the death penalty, and never would. And that was essentially what Nina Taylor had become. A self-appointed death penalty for those she believed had evaded the law.

'Boss,' Nick said, breaking her train of thought as he hurried over. Ruth had made it clear to everyone in CID that finding Nina as quickly as possible was vital before she killed someone else.

'Yes,' Ruth said, as her eyes roamed across the scene boards. She prayed that they wouldn't have to add another photo and date of birth to it. Because if they did, she would feel personally responsible.

'Robert Mills,' Nick said, pointing to a printout that he was holding. 'He's the young man we believe Nina was waiting for when she followed and killed Felix Monroe instead.'

Oh shit!

Ruth had already caught up with Nick's train of thought. 'We're assuming that Nina will be trying to get out of Chester and make her escape. But what if instead she decides to go after more victims until we catch her?'

'Exactly.' Nick nodded. 'And my assumption is that Robert Mills would be first on that list.'

'That sounds about right.' Ruth gave him a concerned look. 'Except Nina has a head start on us. Got an address?'

Nick held up the printout. 'Terraced house in the city centre. From what I can see, he's freelance and works from home. I've called to see if a uniformed patrol car can get over there asap.'

'We'd better get going in case they don't get there quickly enough,' Ruth said, as they turned and hurried for the doors.

194

Chapter 48

Nina had managed to manoeuvre her suit jacket sleeves down a little so that her handcuffs were now covered. However, it wouldn't be long before one of the patrol cars that were currently speeding around the city centre with blue lights flashing spotted her. Either that, or they'd see her on one of the many CCTV cameras. The first thing she needed to do was get the handcuffs off. And then radically change her appearance.

Having worked for the CPS for more than a decade, Nina had come across her fair share of resourceful criminals. Several times she had seen female criminals just slip handcuffs off because their hands and wrists were so small, or they were double jointed. It was a neat trick, but one she was struggling to replicate. She'd spent the past ten minutes standing behind a row of tall hedgerows in Grosvenor Park in the centre of Chester beside the River Dee, pulling and twisting at her cuffs to no avail. It wouldn't be long before someone spotted what she was doing, think her behaviour suspicious, and call the police.

Twice, Nina had seen footage from CCTV in a police

station of female criminals escaping from cuffs by smearing Vaseline under them and pulling. The cuffs slipped off their wrists as if by magic.

Realising that this was now her only option, she left the park, walked past the Roman ruins of an amphitheatre and headed into the city centre. Despite walking with her hands dropped down in front of her because of the handcuffs, no one seemed to notice or pay her any attention.

Spotting a large chemist and makeup shop, she went inside and pretended to casually browse for makeup before going over to where the Vaseline was kept. She assumed that because she was wearing a smart designer trouser suit, she wouldn't be on anyone's radar as a typical shoplifter. Popping the tub of Vaseline into her pocket, she made sure her sleeves were over the cuffs again and strolled casually towards the exit.

Now out on the main shopping street in the middle of Chester, she crossed the road and entered a bar. She pretended to be looking for someone as she moved towards the ladies toilets, which she knew were at the back.

Checking to make sure the toilets were empty, Nina went in the first available cubicle and slid the lock across. She spent the next five minutes switching the pot of Vaseline backwards and forwards between her hands, using her fingers to deposit as much as she could under and around the cuffs.

When she was satisfied that she was finished, she took a deep breath and pulled and twisted the cuffs as hard as she could. She watched them slip on the Vaseline but then stop as they came to the hard, almost circular bumps of her wrist bones.

Shit!

She pulled again with everything she had.

Nothing. They were still stuck.

Starting to panic, she wondered what the hell she was going to do instead.

Fuck it. One more try, she told herself.

Wincing at the pain of the cuffs cutting into her wrists, Nina pulled and pulled. It was agony.

Come on, you've got to do this, however much it hurts.

Suddenly, the cuffs slipped and clattered noisily to the floor.

Thank God for that, she thought as she massaged the sore, red, slippery skin. *That is seriously fucking painful!*

She used toilet roll to clean the Vaseline from her fingers, hands and wrists. Then she picked the cuffs up from the floor and popped them into her pocket, making a mental note to dispose of them somewhere they wouldn't ever be found. She didn't want the police to know she'd managed to get them off.

As she came out of the cubicle, she saw two women in their 30s coming through the door.

'Hi there,' she said in a friendly tone, and left.

A few minutes later, she was looking at racks of clothes in a high street shop. Checking that the items she had picked didn't have security tags, she made her way towards the changing rooms.

She pulled on a navy-coloured hoodie with a logo, a black baseball cap, black trackies and trainers, then popped on a pair of sunglasses to finish the look. She glanced at her reflection, confident that she couldn't possibly look any more different to the woman who had just escaped from the courthouse.

They're just idiots, she told herself. *And you are always going to be one step ahead of them.*

She took the sunglasses off and put them in her pocket. As she came out of the changing rooms, a shop assistant came over.

'Everything okay?' the young woman asked.

'Fine, great,' Nina said with a confident smile. Then she gestured to the changing rooms. 'Can you do me a favour? I've left my bag and business suit in there, but I just need to go and show my husband these clothes. Could you just keep an eye on them for me? I'll only be a minute.'

'Of course,' the young woman assured her. 'I'm going to be around here, so don't worry.'

'Thank you,' Nina said, looking at her with a grateful smile. 'That's very helpful.'

Then she waltzed casually towards the exit, out onto the high street, and put the sunglasses back on.

Well, that was easy.

As she turned onto the cobbled pedestrianised part of central Chester, two uniformed police officers – a man and woman in their 20s – walked towards her.

Shit!

She held her breath.

She glanced around, looking for a place where she could make her escape.

The officers walked straight past her, oblivious to who she was. Her new clothes had worked a treat!

Right, now for the main event, she thought, but realised that she didn't have a weapon.

Over to her left was a very posh-looking kitchenware shop – pots, pans and very expensive knives. In the same casual way as before, she managed to give the owner a friendly smile and then a minute later take a knife from a knife-block on display, put it into her pocket and leave the shop without being detected.

Cutting down past Chester Cathedral, Nina soon found herself at the small terraced house where she knew her next victim lived.

She glanced up and down the road to check that no

one was around. Then she pushed the doorbell and waited. She could feel her pulse racing and her mouth was dry. She was aware that every time she killed, the more addictive it became.

Her fingers wrapped around the handle of the knife as she pulled it slowly from her pocket and let it hang innocuously by her side.

A few seconds later, the door opened and a young man in his 20s looked at her and frowned.

'Bet you don't recognise me, do you?' Nina said with a friendly smile as she took off her sunglasses. 'We met at Chester Crown Court at the beginning of the year?'

The young man shook his head and shrugged. 'Sorry, I …'

Nina gestured. 'Mind if I come in?'

The young man looked baffled. 'I … erm … I'm just …'

She plunged the knife straight into his stomach and pushed him backwards into his house.

Nina kicked the front door closed behind her and then looked down at the man who had fallen to the floor, clutching his stomach which was now bleeding profusely.

'It's all right,' she reassured him. 'I just thought I'd come in for a chat.'

'You need to help me,' he groaned as he looked down at his hands that were awash with bright red blood.

'I don't think so,' Nina snorted as she stood over him. 'I'm going to watch you suffer and die slowly. And while you're doing that, you can think about Harriet Bailey and all you put her through that night.'

Chapter 49

Ruth and Nick sped down the residential street close to the centre of Chester with their siren and the blue lights at the front of their 2-litre Astra flashing.

Nick pulled the car to a sudden halt outside the small, terraced house – the address they'd got for Robert Mills. A few passers-by looked on anxiously, wondering what all the commotion was about.

Getting quickly out of the car, Ruth and Nick jogged over to the front door and pressed the bell.

Without even waiting for an answer, Nick moved to his right and cupped his hands as he tried to look inside the house.

'Anything?' Ruth asked.

Nick shook his head. 'No, nothing.'

Crouching down, Ruth pushed open the letterbox and looked inside. All she could see was the hall carpet stretching away, and the doorway to what looked like a kitchen.

She couldn't see or hear anything.

Then she heard footsteps coming down the stairs.

'Mr Mills?' she called loudly through the letterbox. 'Can you open your front door? It's the police.'

Silence.

Ruth exchanged a look with Nick. 'Well, there's definitely someone in there. I've just seen them come down the stairs.'

Nick gave her a dark look. 'Unless we're too late.'

Ruth rang the doorbell again.

Silence.

Something didn't feel right.

'You think she's in there?' Nick asked quietly.

Before Ruth could answer, there was the sound of a key being turned in the lock and the door opened very slowly.

A well-dressed man in his 20s peered out, looking scared. 'Hi ... can I help?'

'Robert Mills?' Ruth asked.

'Yes,' he replied, looking completely baffled.

Ruth and Nick showed him their warrant cards. 'DI Hunter and DS Evans, Llancastell CID. We need to come in to talk to you about something. It's urgent.'

'Erm, right, okay,' Mills said as he opened the door looking somewhat bemused by their urgency.

They came into the hallway of a small but very tastefully decorated house. Even though it was tidy, it also had all the hallmarks of being 'a bachelor pad'.

'Have you seen the news?' Ruth asked.

'Yes,' Mills replied, 'that's why I hesitated to open the door,' he explained.

'Right,' Nick said. 'Well, we think your life is in danger, so we're going to have to take you into protective custody.'

'What?' Mills gave them a baffled look. 'I don't understand.'

'We believe that Nina Taylor, the woman who has

escaped from custody in Chester, is going to target you. So we need you to come with us right now.'

'That's ridiculous,' he snorted in a slightly pompous tone. 'Why on earth would she target me?'

'You were arrested and charged with indecent assault and the attempted rape of a sixteen-year-old girl just over a year ago—' Ruth started to explain.

'But those charges were all dropped a few weeks ago,' Mills protested, interrupting her.

'Yes,' Ruth said, 'and that's why we believe she is going to target you.'

Mills shook his head. 'I'm still lost.'

Nick looked at him. 'We believe that Nina Taylor is targeting anyone who was charged with committing that type of offence but then didn't proceed to a criminal trial.'

'Jesus …' Mills muttered, looking horrified.

'If you can get some things together in an overnight bag,' Ruth said calmly, 'then we need you to come with us.'

Mills now appeared genuinely scared by what they'd told him.

'Right, give me five minutes and I'll be with you,' he said as he jogged upstairs.

Ruth then looked at Nick. 'If she didn't come here, then where the hell did she go?'

Chapter 50

Opening the fridge, Nina took out some milk and headed over to the kettle where she was making herself a cup of tea. James Symes had finally died on the carpet of his house about ten minutes earlier. She'd enjoyed watching him squirm and plead for her to help him as he bled out. It was fascinating to watch the colour slowly drain from his face as his life faded away. It was no less than he deserved. And on top of that, Nina had saved some other poor woman who James would have undoubtedly attacked at some point in the future. It was inevitable. It was like that Tom Cruise film, 'Minority Report', where he plays a cop who arrests people for crimes that they were going to commit in the future. That's what she was doing. Men like James Symes would go on to attack and force themselves on other women in the future. She was just preventing that from happening.

Taking her tea from the kitchen, she stepped over Symes' body which now lay in a huge congealing pool of blood. Then she had a walk around the house to see what might be useful for her to take. She had already found a set of car keys for a VW Golf hanging in the kitchen. She took a quick peek through the downstairs window and saw that a virtually brand new, black, four-door Golf was parked outside. A quick click of a button on the fob was followed by the car's indicators flashing.

Okay, so now I've got a nice car, she thought.

As she continued to wander around, her thoughts turned to DI Ruth Hunter. It wouldn't be long before she found James Symes' case and saw that the charges had been dropped.

DI Hunter was a curiosity to her. From what she'd heard, she was a gay woman who lived with her partner. Didn't that make her the ultimate believer in female empowerment? Nina didn't understand why she didn't get what Nina was doing. Surely DI Hunter had seen too many men who she knew were guilty of horrible crimes walk free? Didn't that get to her? Didn't it make her angry? Didn't she think that there was another way of doing things? Surely she could see that women needed to dish out their own brand of justice. It was the only way for society to be a safe place for everyone.

Grabbing a bag from upstairs, Nina went into Symes' bathroom and looked in the cabinet. There was some black hair dye for men. He clearly didn't want anyone to know that he was going prematurely grey. She popped the hair dye into the bag – it might come in useful.

Coming downstairs, she took some food, drink, a rain-coat, Symes' mobile phone and his wallet. She spotted a pair of designer reading glasses and took those too.

Right, all set, she thought as she went to the front door and gave James Symes one last look. She felt an over-whelming sense of satisfaction at a job well done.

It was now on to her next victim.

Neston? Maybe I'll take a trip to Neston, she thought as she closed the front door and headed for the car.

Chapter 51

Ruth had called together everyone from Chester Town Hall nick CID, along with her own detectives from Llancastell. The investigation seemed to be moving at pace, with several major developments that everyone needed to be brought up to speed with. The CID office was now hot and stuffy, despite several large fans blowing noisily in the far corner. Taking a swig of water from her bottle, Ruth blew out her cheeks.

Christ, it's like an oven in here, she thought.

'Right, listen up everyone,' she said, trying to muster as much energy as she could. 'I have another press conference in about an hour. I need us to circulate Nina Taylor's photograph to as many media outlets as we can. Every police officer in the Cheshire, North Wales and Wirral areas has been given a description and photo too. What I need from you, are ideas about where she might be heading.'

Kennedy looked over. 'Boss, Nina's family are from Neston on the Wirral. According to the electoral register, her parents still live there.'

'Right, I need a plain clothes unit stationed at that house,' Ruth said. 'If Nina decides to make contact, we need someone to be there. What else have we got?'

Nick signalled to her. 'What about other cases that the CPS dropped recently in Chester or North Wales?'

'My instinct is that Nina will be trying to track down and kill as many men as she can who she believes haven't been brought to justice for attacking women,' Ruth said. 'We need a definitive list. Any men in Cheshire and North Wales who have been arrested and charged with sexual assault or rape in the past two years, who have had those charges against them dropped in the past three months.' She looked out at the team. 'Let's get one step ahead of her. I don't want her to take any more lives, so we have to find her. And fast.'

Chapter 52

It was early evening by the time Ruth looked out at the packed press room with some trepidation. She couldn't believe that she was having to hold two press conferences in the same day, but given all that had happened it was vital that the media were aware of all that was going on. And she certainly didn't want the UK media running their own ill-informed stories based on rumours or tip-offs. What was now more of a concern were the TV crews from US television stations such as NBC, and the main Australian news channel, ABC. The idea that this was becoming an international news story made Ruth feel very uneasy. Due to the short notice and timing, she didn't even have the reassurance of a police media officer by her side. She was out there on her own.

Taking a deep breath to compose herself, Ruth looked out at the room. *Come on, Ruth, you've got this.*

'Good evening, I'm Detective Inspector Ruth Hunter and I am the senior investigating officer on the Nina Taylor case. I want to update you on developments in this case in the last twelve hours. Our primary concern is the safety of the public primarily in the Cheshire and North Wales area.' Ruth took a moment and sipped her water. Now she had started, her nerves were under control. 'This morning, Nina Taylor escaped from police custody after a bail hearing at Cheshire Crown Court. She was awaiting transportation to HMP Tonsgrove on Anglesey. All measures and precautions had been taken with regards to security, and it was an extraordinary set of circumstances that led to her escape. Our thoughts are with the families of the victims of these horrific crimes at what must be a very difficult time.' Ruth cleared her throat and then continued. 'We are absolutely committed to finding Nina Taylor and we are using every resource available to us to bring our search to a conclusion as quickly as possible. There are currently a number of operations underway in the Cheshire and North Wales area. For obvious reasons, I am unable to explain where or what those operations are. However, I do have a few minutes for some questions, if anyone has any?'

As she feared, a dozen or so hands shot up from around the room.

A young male journalist at the front of the room indicated he wanted to ask a question and Ruth nodded in his direction. 'Jonathan Holmes, Daily Express. Can you explain to our readers how Nina Taylor, a dangerous, violent killer, was allowed to escape while being escorted by both prison and police officers. That seems extremely negligent and has put the public in danger.'

'I'm not at liberty to give details of Nina Taylor's escape yesterday. However, the incident will be investigated thoroughly. We have also voluntarily referred this to the IOPC, and we will fully cooperate with their independent investigation and any rulings.' Ruth knew this wasn't what the journalist was looking for, but no one was going to tell the press how Nina had got away.

Ruth pointed to a television journalist who was standing towards the back of the room. 'Tracy Adams, BBC News. Can you tell us what resources you have available in the search for Nina Taylor and whether you believe they are adequate?'

Ruth nodded. 'We have over fifty police officers working on this case. We have received resources in terms of officers, vehicles and expertise, from Merseyside, Cheshire, North Wales and Shropshire Police forces. I would like to thank my colleagues from across the country for their ongoing support.' Ruth then got up and collected her folders from the table. 'I'm afraid that's all I have time for now. Thank you for your cooperation.'

Ruth turned and headed for the exit with a sigh of relief.

Chapter 53

It was gone 7pm as Ruth sat back in the padded DI's chair and tried to take five minutes to get her head straight. There was a television on silently in the CID office. The BBC News channel was featuring the search for Nina as one of their headlines. It featured an aerial shot of central Chester along with photos of Nina with the strapline – *Search continues for Nina Taylor, wanted by police in connection with three murders. Police have warned that she is dangerous and is not to be approached.*

Nick poked his head in.

'Come and sit down for a second,' Ruth said with a gesture.

He sat down and gave her a dispirited look. 'We've got nothing so far. A few crank calls saying Nina's been seen in Stoke and Liverpool. Otherwise, nothing. We've trawled the CCTV from Chester city centre, but so far we've drawn a blank.'

Ruth gave a frustrated sigh. 'Anything from that unit over in Neston?'

'No.' Nick shook his head. 'If she had transport, or

arranged for someone to pick her up, she could be a couple of hundred miles away by now.'

'She's effectively vanished,' Ruth groaned.

'Anything from Superintendent Rickson?' Nick asked.

'No. And I'm trying to avoid him for obvious reasons,' Ruth admitted. 'But he's going to want to talk to me at some point tonight.'

Ruth's phone rang. She had hoped it was Sarah with some good news about Daniel's adoption. Instead, it was a number that she didn't recognise.

'DI Ruth Hunter,' she said as she answered it.

'Ruth?' said a friendly voice. It was a woman, but she couldn't place her.

'Hello?' Ruth said in a quizzical tone.

'It's Nina,' said the voice.

What?

Ruth sat up in her chair as her stomach tightened. Then she frantically gestured to Nick. 'Oh hi, Nina.'

Nick's eyes widened in shock.

'Just thought I'd check in to see how things are going,' Nina said.

'Yeah, I didn't recognise the number,' Ruth explained, keeping the slightly strange upbeat tone of the conversation going.

'Oh, so you haven't found him then?' Nina asked, sounding surprised.

'Found who?' Ruth asked, wondering who she was talking about and fearing the worst.

'James Symes.'

Ruth gestured to Nick that he needed to write down what she was saying. 'James Symes? I don't think we're aware of a James Symes.'

Nick scribbled the name down and then signalled to

Ruth that he was going to go and research the name immediately.

'Oh dear. Well, you will do. Nasty piece of work. Deserved everything he got,' Nina said in a conceited tone. 'I just thought if you'd found James, you'd have his mobile phone number.'

Ruth's heart sank at what Nina said. She had clearly killed James Symes and now there was yet another victim in her terrible killing spree.

'Where are you, Nina?' Ruth asked in a nonchalant tone.

'Nice try,' Nina laughed. 'A long, long way from you. I'm going to be out of the country by tomorrow, so I thought I'd ring to say goodbye.'

Ruth racked her brain. How was Nina going to get out of the country without a passport, and with every airport and ferry port on high alert?

'I'm surprised you're able to travel,' Ruth said, seeing if she could prompt Nina into revealing a clue as to where she was going.

'Friends in high places,' she said. 'That's all you need to know. You'll find out soon enough.'

'So, I'm guessing that your work is done then?'

'Far from it,' Nina said, and then her tone changed to one of anger. 'I'm really surprised at you, Ruth. I had you down as someone who would be all for 'female empowerment'.'

'I am,' Ruth replied. 'Just not senseless murder.'

'Senseless?' Nina scoffed. 'How can you possibly say what I've done is senseless? You've seen the social media stuff. I'm a female heroine. #Ninatakingbackthepower.'

Ruth had seen the growing online support for what Nina had done and it was terrifying. And it had allowed her to become deluded into thinking that her actions were justified.

'You can't tell me that taking those animals off the planet wasn't a positive thing to do,' Nina said in a withering tone. 'You've seen all sorts of men who you know are guilty released back on to the streets and then commit more horrendous crimes. Doesn't that keep you awake at night? Doesn't it make you angry?'

'It does make me angry, Nina,' Ruth said, worried that she was now being drawn into some kind of moral debate. But the longer she kept Nina talking, the more likely it was that the phone she was using would register on one of the telecom masts. And from those masts, the digital forensics team could triangulate the signal and give Ruth a fairly precise location of where the phone was. The results weren't always immediate, but any clue as to where Nina was calling from was vital.

'But you're going to hunt me down and put me in prison,' Nina protested.

'You've committed murder,' Ruth said sternly, 'and you followed and killed an innocent man in Felix Monroe. You can't possibly justify that.'

'It's what our government calls 'collateral damage' in any war,' she retorted. 'And don't make any bones about this, this is a war, Ruth.'

'I'm afraid I don't see it like that.'

'That's very disappointing. How would you feel if someone did that to your daughter?'

'My daughter was kidnapped a couple of years ago. It terrified her,' Ruth recalled, 'but I never thought that killing the man who did it was the right thing to do.'

'That makes you naïve,' Nina sneered. 'You're part of the problem. What if you had a son?'

'I do have a son,' Ruth said. She counted Daniel as her son, whatever happened in the future.

'I didn't know that.'

'Daniel,' Ruth stated, but instantly regretted telling Nina personal information, however innocuous that seemed.

'What are you going to tell him? How are you going to get Daniel to respect girls and women as he grows up, when he's surrounded by images, films, music and his peers who denigrate women?'

'My partner and I will explain to him how to treat girls and women with the utmost respect as he grows up,' Ruth said, annoyed that they were even having this conversation.

'You can't do that,' Nina scoffed. 'It's in his DNA. He's doomed to mistreat women as he grows up. They're all doomed, I'm afraid. Men are obsolete and there's no place for them in modern society.'

'You can't honestly believe that.'

Nick came back in and looked at her. She nodded to confirm that Nina was still on the phone.

'Anyway, I can't talk to you all day.' Nina laughed and ended the call.

'Nina?' Ruth said, and then glanced at Nick. 'I kept her on the phone as long as I could. I'm afraid she's a very sick person. Utterly deluded.'

French came to the door and knocked on it. 'Boss, we've got a report of a man stabbed in his home in central Chester.'

'Have you got a name?' she asked, fearing the worst.

'James Symes,' he said.

Chapter 54

Ruth and Nick pulled up outside James Symes' home in a quiet residential street just north of Chester Cathedral. Uniformed officers had already pulled their cars across the road to stop traffic. The area around the front door and pavement had been cordoned off with blue and white evidence tape. Across the road about a dozen neighbours and onlookers were standing watching, trying to work out what had happened. Directly outside Symes' house was a forensic van that belonged to the SOCOs. Its back doors were open and a SOCO in full nitrile forensic suit, hat and mask, was putting evidence away inside.

Walking towards a young officer who was manning the cordon and keeping the neighbours away, Ruth got out her warrant card.

'DI Hunter and DS Evans, CID,' she said.

'What have we got, constable?' Nick asked.

The officer looked down at his notebook. 'Daisy Gower, the victim's girlfriend, had arranged to have a coffee with him this morning. When he didn't show up and didn't answer his phone, she came round and knocked on the door. When she looked through the window, she saw him lying on the floor,' he explained. 'So, she called us.'

'What did you find?' Ruth asked.

'We broke the front door down but Mr Symes was already deceased, ma'am. There was nothing we could do,' he said, looking slightly haunted by recalling what he'd seen. 'There was a stab wound to the abdomen. By the looks of it, he bled to death.'

'Any sign of forced entry?' Nick enquired.

'No, sir.'

'Start running a scene log, please. No one comes onto the crime scene without my say so,' said Ruth.

'Yes, ma'am.'

The officer pulled up the police tape and Ruth and Nick headed for the house.

As they arrived, they showed their warrant cards and a SOCO handed each of them a full forensic suit. They rustled noisily and smelled of chemicals. Ruth could still remember when CID officers just popped on some gloves and trod all over crime scenes in the 90s.

Snapping on her blue latex gloves, Ruth gestured for Nick to follow her inside. There were already aluminium stepping plates on the carpet of the hallway as they went in.

Lying in the hallway was James Symes. Not only was he covered in blood, there was also a huge pool of blood around his body.

Several SOCOs were dusting surfaces and examining the carpet for forensic evidence. Another SOCO was taking photographs.

Even though they knew who had murdered Symes, they needed as much evidence as they could get for when Nina Taylor was eventually arrested and brought to trial.

Nick made his way further into the house and into the kitchen.

A figure in a white forensic suit approached Ruth and pulled down their mask. It was Professor Barnes.

'Hello Inspector,' she said, as she tried to avoid the pool of blood.

'Hello … Bit of a mess,' Ruth said, pointing to the floor.

'I assume this is Nina Taylor's doing?' Barnes said quietly.

'I'm afraid so.'

'She stabbed him and then waited for him to bleed out. Horrible way to die.' She then gave Ruth a slightly haughty look. 'I just hope you catch her before she does this to someone else.'

She pulled up her mask and wandered away.

Ruth got a strong sense that Barnes' comment was intended to imply that James Symes' murder was her fault for allowing Nina to escape from custody. That had already occurred to Ruth, and she was feeling guilty enough without Barnes rubbing salt into the wound.

Ruth took out her phone and called French.

'Hi, boss,' he said as he answered.

'We're at James Symes' house,' Ruth said. 'It's now an absolute priority that we find every man who has had sexual assault or rape charges dropped in North Wales or Cheshire and take them into protective custody. I suggest you go and commandeer uniformed officers to help. That has got to happen today, Dan.'

'No problem, boss,' he reassured her. 'We've found four so far and two have been contacted and moved to safety.'

'Good.' Ruth felt a sense of relief that French was on the case and working fast. He had been such a valuable member of the CID team at Llancastell over the years.

'That's great work, Dan. Let me know when the other two have been found.'

'Will do, boss,' he replied, and ended the call.

Nick approached. He was holding something.

'What have you got?' she asked him.

He held up an evidence bag with what looked like a car log book inside – it had a large VW badge on.

'Symes owns a brand new Golf,' he said, gesturing to the log book.

'And?' Ruth asked.

'There's a key rack in the kitchen but no car keys, and I've looked up and down the road and there's not a Golf in sight.'

'You think that Nina's taken his car?' Ruth asked.

'I think it's very likely. If we contact the manufacturer, we might be able to track the Golf's GPS signal.'

Ruth felt a surge of hope. It might just be the break-through they needed.

Chapter 55

It was nearly 7.30pm as Ruth stood in front of the scene boards back in the CID office. She had called everyone in both CID teams together again before packing them off to go home for a shower, food, a few hours' sleep and then back in again. It wasn't unusual with a case like this for detectives to survive for days on tiny amounts of sleep. Ruth had arranged for a skeleton staff to continue to run the investigation overnight but she expected the team back in the early hours.

'Right guys,' she said, aware that she was now feeling exhausted. She had noticed that since she'd been shot and had a cardiac arrest, her energy reserves were depleted. Her consultant had explained that was normal and it could take many months for her to get back to full health. 'It's been quite a day, to say the least. And I know most of you are running on empty. So, as I explained earlier, some of you are going to stay. I want everyone else to go home, eat, shower and sleep. I need all of you to be sharp and full of energy if we're going to catch Nina Taylor …' Ruth looked around the room. 'What do I need to know before we go?'

Nick looked over. 'I've spoken to Volkswagon but it's going to take several hours for them to track down the GPS for that Golf and then give us the authorisation to track it. Could even be tomorrow lunchtime.'

'Shit!' Ruth said under her breath in frustration. 'We don't have until tomorrow lunchtime. God knows what that maniac is going to do next. What about the phone signal?'

Kennedy raised her pen to show that she had been dealing with it. 'Digital forensics are working on it. But again, probably nothing until the morning either, boss.'

'Okay,' Ruth sighed. 'I want that car's registration distributed to all units. And I want traffic to run a continual ANPR check for it overnight.'

'I've spoken to them, boss,' French said, 'and that's all in place now.'

Ruth turned and pointed to a photo of Nina. 'She has to be going somewhere. Any ideas?'

'We have a unit stationed at her home in Buckley,' Kennedy said, 'but I don't think she's stupid enough to even try returning there.'

'No, neither do I,' Ruth agreed.

French sat forward in his seat. 'All four men who had charges against them dropped have been contacted and taken into protective custody. If she's targeting them, then that's a non-starter.'

Nick raised an eyebrow. 'She's not stupid. Won't she know that we will have tracked down those men by now?'

'Maybe, but I still want uniformed patrols to keep an eye on all of their properties. If she does go after them, I don't want us to miss her. She did mention that she was going to be leaving the country,' Ruth explained. 'She told me that she has 'friends in high places.' I don't know what she meant by that, and I don't know how she thinks she's going anywhere without a passport.'

'Ferry to Dublin?' Nick suggested.

Ruth nodded. She'd worked a couple of cases before when criminals had made a break for Holyhead on Anglesey to get a ferry across the Irish Sea to Dublin. For some reason, there was no requirement to show a valid passport for that journey. 'That's one possibility. But we do have uniformed patrols at Holyhead, and the security officers have been given Nina's photograph and description.'

'We've trawled through friends and family,' Georgie said, 'but there's nothing obvious there.'

'Okay,' Ruth said, as she glanced at her watch. 'Right, I want everyone apart from the skeleton staff to go home right now. I will be doing the same but I aim to be back in here around 2am. Thanks for all your hard work today. Now bugger off.'

Chapter 56

Ruth parked her car on the drive at her home in Bangor-on-Dee and took a moment. *Right, first thing I need is a huge glass of wine and a ciggie*, she thought to herself as she unclipped her seatbelt and opened the driver's door. She went across the small path that dissected her tidy front garden and took out her keys. Looking up, she saw that even though it was 8.30pm, it was only just starting to get dark. The sky above was a lovely shade of indigo with the faintest dots of stars that had started to appear. It didn't look real.

Ruth unlocked the door and shouted, 'Hello?' as she went in.

'Hello?' came the response from Sarah. From the direction of her voice, Ruth guessed she was in the living room.

Ruth kicked off her shoes and wriggled her toes into the thick carpet as she padded down the hallway towards the kitchen.

'Wine?' she called out.

'Awwww,' Sarah called back, clearly making a joke on the word 'whine'.

'Bloody comedian,' Ruth grumbled, noticing that she was feeling tetchy. She needed to have a word with herself. 'Do I take that as a 'yes' then?'

'If you are,' Sarah responded.

'If I don't have a drink, my head is going to explode,' Ruth shouted as she opened the fridge, pulled out a bottle of Sauvignon Blanc and plonked it down on the counter. Then she grabbed two glasses that were the size of fish bowls, twisted the top off the wine and poured two large glasses. Then she returned the bottle to the fridge, noticing that they had virtually half a bottle in just two glasses.

Ruth took the glasses and made her way into the living room where Sarah was slumped on the sofa watching television.

'Here you go, treacle,' Ruth said, exaggerating her London accent as she handed a glass to Sarah.

'Treacle?' Sarah asked as she pulled a face.

'It's what my dad used to call me. And my mum. Normally when he wanted something,' Ruth explained as she sat down.

'There's a social worker here,' Sarah said as she sipped her wine.

Ruth frowned. 'Where?'

'Oh, Daniel is showing her the garden. Where he planted those sunflowers,' Sarah explained. 'I told her that you'd messaged to say that you'd be home by 8.30pm so she said she'd wait.'

'Do you mean Susannah?' Ruth asked, now frustrated that she couldn't go and have a crafty ciggie in the garden. Maybe she'd go out the front door and hide.

'No, it's a different woman. She seems very nice. Alice I think she said her name was. I assume it's something to do with the application.'

'Right,' Ruth said, thinking that she needed wine, food, shower and sleep.

Sarah noticed Ruth's expression. 'I'm sure it won't take very long.'

'It's fine,' Ruth sighed. 'I'm just cream crackered.'

Sarah laughed. 'Something else your dad used to say I suppose?'

'Yes,' Ruth replied with a smile.

Sarah got up, went over to the sliding patio doors which were open by about two feet and went outside.

Ruth closed her eyes but it was hard to think about anything other than Nina Taylor out there somewhere planning her next move. And it was Ruth's fault that she was on the loose.

'I can't find them,' Sarah said, looking puzzled as she came back inside.

'What do you mean?' Ruth asked, opening her eyes and realising that she might have dozed off for a second or two.

Sarah gestured to the garden. 'They're not out there. They've disappeared.'

What?

Ruth got up from the chair and looked over at the hallway. 'Maybe Daniel has taken her to go and see his bedroom?'

'He can't have done,' Sarah said, now sounding worried. 'I would have heard them.'

Ruth's pulse started to quicken. She moved swiftly into the garden and looked around.

Nothing.

Panic set in.

The garden wasn't big enough for anyone to hide in.

Where the hell are they.

SIMON MCCLEAVE

'I'll check upstairs,' Ruth said, her mind whirring and her stomach tight.

'Where have they gone?' Sarah exclaimed, her eyes full of fear as she followed Ruth inside.

'It's fine,' Ruth reassured her but she was now scared. 'They can't have gone far.'

Running up the stairs, Ruth went along the landing and looked in Daniel's bedroom.

Nothing.

She looked at the place on his desk where he always left his mobile phone to charge – it wasn't there.

This is starting to worry me, she thought to herself trying to keep composed.

'Is he up there?' Sarah shouted.

Ruth went from room to room but neither Daniel nor Alice the social worker were anywhere to be seen.

'No,' Ruth replied as she thundered down the stairs. Then something occurred to her. 'Where was her car?'

'What?' Sarah asked.

'This Alice. When I parked on the drive, there weren't any cars parked on the road,' Ruth said, her heart now beating fast. 'Where was her car?'

'I don't know,' Sarah muttered nervously. Then she looked at Ruth. 'Where are they?'

Ruth's mind was whirring. She took out her phone and rang Daniel's phone. It started to ring.

'His phone is ringing,' Ruth said, aware that it wasn't anywhere in the house. 'He must have it with him.'

'Why isn't he answering it?'

'Did this Alice show you any ID?' Ruth asked.

'No,' Sarah gasped, 'but she knew our names. She knew Daniel lived here. She looked like a social worker.'

'Describe her,' Ruth said as another dark, terrible thought had crossed her mind.

Nina Taylor.

They had spoken about Daniel that afternoon. Not only was Nina angry with Ruth, she also believed that all men were doomed to treat women badly. In her warped mind, had Nina taken Daniel to prove some point?

'She was medium height, slim, 40s,' Sarah gabbled anxiously.

'What colour was her hair?' Ruth asked, remembering Nina's tousled blonde locks.

'Black,' Sarah replied looking at Ruth suspiciously. 'And she was wearing glasses.'

That doesn't add up.

'Black? Are you sure?' Ruth asked.

'Yes, black. But it looked like it had been dyed black,' Sarah said frantically. 'Why are you asking me this?'

Ruth didn't answer for a few seconds. She was trying to piece everything together.

'Who do you think it was?' Sarah demanded.

Ruth looked at her. 'I spoke to Nina Taylor this afternoon …'

'What?' The colour drained from Sarah's face.

'And we spoke about Daniel very briefly.'

'Why?' Sarah asked with a pained expression.

'I don't know, we just did,' Ruth said. 'But Nina Taylor is blonde, and she doesn't wear glasses.'

Then Ruth remembered the small tattoo of a flower between the base of Nina's thumb and her wrist.

'What about a tattoo?' Ruth asked.

'What?'

'Did you notice any tattoos?'

'Yes.' Sarah turned her hand and pointed. 'She had a flower tattoo just here. It's exactly where I want one.'

Ruth's stomach lurched as she took a breath to steady herself.

'What? What is it?' Sarah asked, now standing right in front of Ruth.

Ruth gave her a dark look as she felt sick with horror. 'It was her. It was Nina Taylor. She's got Daniel.'

Chapter 57

Having tried to calm Sarah down, Ruth had driven straight back to the CID office at Chester Town Hall police station, calling Nick and the others on the way. They were all heading in.

It was now 12am and Ruth was sitting in the DI's office feeling utterly overwhelmed by anxiety and fear.

Nick came in and handed her a coffee. 'Here you go.'

'Thanks,' Ruth said quietly. She just couldn't concentrate.

Nick looked directly at her and placed a comforting hand on her shoulder. 'We are going to get Daniel back safely. I promise you.'

Ruth nodded. 'Thank you.' She wished she could share his optimism. She got up and wandered out into the CID office. She stared over at the scene boards and the photo of Nina Taylor, still with her blonde hair. Ruth couldn't help but blame herself. If she hadn't entered into the conversation about Daniel with Nina, he would be tucked up in bed at home.

'Boss,' Georgie said, pointing at her screen.

'What is it?' Ruth asked, as she wandered over to see what Georgie was looking at.

On Georgie's screen was the front page of a tabloid newspaper. It featured a photo of a man with a pug nose and a shaved head. The headline was – *FACE OF A MONSTER!*

'What's that?' Ruth asked, wondering what the relevance was.

'In 2001, Nina Taylor was raped by this man, Kevin Green. She was fourteen at the time. Green then raped and murdered Nina's five-year-old sister,' Georgie explained.

'What?' Ruth exclaimed, wide-eyed.

'It gets worse. Green appealed against his life sentence. His defence team found that several officers had tampered with evidence. He was released after only serving 18 months.'

'Dear God,' Ruth said. 'I remember that case. It was when I was in the Met. I had no idea that was Nina and her sister.'

'Where's Kevin Green now?' Nick asked.

'He died from cancer three years ago,' Georgie said.

'So, she can't be going after him,' Ruth said, thinking out loud. 'Keep digging and see if there's anything else. It might be relevant to what her next plans are.'

French came in through the doors looking energised. 'Boss, we've got a hit from the GPS on James Symes' mobile phone.' He led them over to the map of the area on the wall and pointed. 'It's located at a motorway services off the M54 on the way to Telford. It's also got a Premier Inn on site and the phone has been stationary for the past hour.'

Ruth got a jolt of nervous energy as she looked at them all. 'Right, let's get down there.'

Chapter 58

It was 2am by the time Ruth and Nick had parked on the far side of the car park at the Telford M54 services. Ruth had arranged for an armed response vehicle – an ARV – to meet them there. Nina Taylor was almost certainly armed with at least a knife, and she had kidnapped Daniel. Ruth needed firearms officers to make sure that he was rescued safely. There were also several patrol cars on standby in case Nina tried to make a run for it, as well as paramedics.

Having left Georgie back at the CID office, Ruth stood behind a huge articulated lorry with Nick, French and Garrow. French had been sent a link to a map by the mobile phone provider, which showed the precise location of James Symes' phone with a blue dot.

The car park was half empty and deserted. In the distance, a couple of lorries and a van had pulled into the petrol station to fill up.

Scouring the car park, Ruth frowned. 'I can't see a VW Golf anywhere,' she whispered.

Nick nodded in agreement. 'Neither can I.'

Ruth pressed the button on her Tetra radio. 'Three six

to all units, we are at the far side of the car park but we have no visual on target vehicle or suspect, over,' she said very quietly.

'Three six, this is Bravo one, receiving, over,' said a crackly voice. Bravo one was the code name for the armed officers.

Ruth, Nick, French and Garrow moved slowly from their cover behind the lorry and then fanned out as they began to move silently through the car park.

The stillness was eerie.

Ruth peered at the parked cars but she still couldn't see the VW Golf that they knew Nina was driving.

Where are you, Daniel? she said to herself. She would give anything to have him back safely in her arms.

There was a metallic clunk from over to her right.

Everyone froze.

It seemed to be coming from a dark grey van.

Ruth looked at the others and signalled for them to head slowly towards where the van was parked.

Another metallic clunk.

Someone is moving around inside that van, Ruth thought to herself.

As they hadn't spotted the VW Golf, she now wondered if Nina had commandeered herself a different vehicle. Nina was smart enough to know that it wouldn't have been long before James Symes' body was discovered, and that his car had been stolen.

Looking at French, Ruth gave him a quizzical look as if to ask where the GPS signal for Symes' mobile phone was coming from.

French pointed – the signal was definitely coming from the vicinity of the grey van.

Maybe Daniel was tied up in the back but was trying to

escape? Maybe that was the noise. Ruth couldn't bear to think of him like that.

Suddenly the side door to the van slid open noisily.

A rotund man in paint-splattered overalls jumped out, rubbed his eyes, and stretched as if he'd been sleeping in the back.

The man turned around, saw them all approaching, and took a step back as his eyes widened in fear.

'Jesus Christ!' he gasped in shock.

Nick flashed his warrant card. 'Police. I'm just going to need you to stay there while I look in your van.'

The man nodded anxiously as he moved to one side.

Ruth joined Nick as they peered into the van. It was full of pots of paint, dust sheets, a step ladder, a single mattress and a blanket.

'It's definitely here,' French said, looking down at the GPS tracker.

Ruth looked around frantically.

The nearest car to them was about thirty yards away.

'Boss,' Garrow said under his breath as he went towards the front of the van. He reached and took something from on top of the tyre.

He held it up. It was an iPhone.

Ruth's heart sank. *Shit!*

The van owner shook his head. 'I didn't know that was there. I swear it's not mine.'

Ruth looked at him and nodded in frustration. 'It's okay, we know it's not yours. Don't worry.'

Nina had tricked them – she was clearly a long way from Telford.

Chapter 59

Nina came out of the hotel room's en suite bathroom where she had washed her face and cleaned her teeth. She felt refreshed. They were in a decent hotel right in the centre of Prestatyn, a seaside resort on the North Wales coast about 30 miles north west of Chester.

She looked over at Daniel who was sitting on the bed with his hands tied behind his back with a plastic tie. She didn't know why, but she felt nothing for him. She was devoid of empathy. She had always wondered if that was a result of being attacked and raped by Kevin Green and what had happened to her sister, Alisha. Had that trauma robbed her of the ability to feel anything? Maybe her whole nervous system had shut down that day. Her counsellor said that she was suffering from night terrors and complex PTSD.

Nina had been in several relationships with men in her 20s and early 30s but it seemed impossible. Her boyfriends had accused her of being cold and distant, especially during sex. She never told them what had happened to her. It was none of their bloody business, and she didn't want their pity. She also feared that if she explained what had happened to her in 2001 they would be repelled, seeing her as damaged goods and reject her.

'Please, just let me go home,' Daniel pleaded, his eyes full of tears.

Nina shook her head. 'I can't do that at the moment, I'm afraid Daniel. There's so much I need to talk to you about and explain. So much to teach you as a young man.'

Walking across the room, Nina grabbed a couple of bags of food that she'd bought from a nearby supermarket using James Symes' credit card. It wouldn't be long before the police were informed of activity on the card and where. That was okay. She wasn't planning on staying there for very long. They needed to be on the road soon.

Nina brandished the knife again. 'If I cut the tie off your hands, you promise not to do anything stupid?'

Daniel nodded emphatically. She was aware that the plastic tie was probably cutting into his skin and very uncomfortable.

'I have this knife still,' Nina warned him.

He bowed his head to signal that he understood.

Nina studied him carefully as she went over to cut him free. 'You haven't got a phone on you or anything silly?'

He shook his head adamantly. 'I had it confiscated by my form tutor at school today,' he said shakily.

'Up you get,' Nina said, as Daniel moved across the bed and rubbed his wrists which were red raw. She knew the feeling. Her wrist bones were still very bruised from where she'd pulled the handcuffs off. 'Arms out either side.'

Daniel grimaced but did as he was told. She gave him a quick pat down to make sure he wasn't lying and then pointed to the bags of food. 'Help yourself to some of that. Go on.'

He walked gingerly over to the bags, grabbed a prepacked sandwich, crisps, and a can of Fanta and sat back on the bed.

Nina drank from a bottle of water and then looked over at Daniel. 'You know the Australian Aborigines have this tradition that they call 'Walkabout'. Teenage boys in the tribe have to leave and go and live on their own in the wilderness, sometimes for a few months. It's supposed to be their spiritual transition into adulthood. Becoming a man. The Maasai of Kenya have a rites of passage for their teenage boys so that they can become 'warriors'. The boys sleep in the forest, learn to fight, hunt, and endure pain. And when they are finished, they are allowed to pick the woman of their choice from the tribe. It's the same all over the world. Patriarchy.' Nina reached for some grapes that were in the bag. Then she turned to Daniel. 'You don't understand what I'm talking about do you?'

Daniel didn't respond. He didn't know what she was getting at. Why should he? She felt sorry for him. To be born a man is to be born with a terrible sense of entitlement and emotional immaturity.

'Don't worry, you're all doomed, Daniel. All men are doomed. From the time you're exposed to the colour-coded childhood of blue and pink. Toy guns, cars and football. Leave the dolls, beauty sets and toy hairdryers for us girls,' Nina continued.

Daniel looked at her nervously as he ate his sandwich tentatively. She watched him but her pity had started to turn to anger. She could see what he was going to become. A predatory man who would believe that the patriarchal society was geared to fulfil his needs. There was no better way of striking a blow for female empowerment than to destroy the boy before he even became that man.

That's it, she thought, as if it were a lighbulb moment.

Sacrifice this man-child sitting across from me to strike fear into the heart of the patriarchy.

For a few seconds, she wondered where she would take Daniel and then it came to her.

'Daniel?' she said, looking over at him.

'Yes?' he replied, as he pulled bits from his sandwich and popped them into his mouth.

'We're going to rest up here for an hour or two,' she explained, as the fully formed plan came together in her mind. 'And then I'm going to take you somewhere. It's somewhere very important to me.'

'Okay,' he said cautiously.

'When I was young … younger than you,' Nina said, 'a horrible man came to my house. He was a friend of my father's. They worked together. But my father and mother were out. And this man hurt me very badly.'

She could see Daniel's face change. He didn't know why she was telling him this story and it was scaring him. But that was the point, wasn't it?

'And then he attacked my little sister. And she was only five,' Nina continued. 'He took her away, killed her, and buried her body.'

Daniel stopped eating. His eyes were teary but he needed to hear what she had to say.

'So, I want to take you somewhere. To a special place,' she said. 'Is that okay?'

Daniel gave the faintest of nods. He was petrified.

She was going to take him to where they had found Alisha. It was symbolic because that was now the place where she was going to kill Daniel and teach the patriarchy a lesson.

Chapter 60

Ruth looked down at her phone. There were several missed calls from Sarah, and messages asking *Any news?* Ruth couldn't help but feel responsible for Daniel's kidnapping. And she knew that Sarah would be out of her mind with worry.

She looked out from the DI's office at the CID team. Even though it was 4am, word had got out about Daniel's abduction and every single detective had raced in to help with the operation to find him.

The BBC News channel was now running the story of Daniel's abduction. Ruth knew how important it was that the public be on the lookout for Nina and Daniel. Often they could be the eyes and ears of the police in a search like this.

Ruth's phone rang. It was Sarah.

'Hi,' Ruth said quietly.

'Anything?' Sarah asked, but Ruth could hear that she was now sounding despondent.

'Sorry,' Ruth said. 'This is my fault.'

'Of course it's not!' she snapped. 'You're not responsible for some psycho kidnapping Daniel.'

Silence.

'What are we going to do?' Sarah asked eventually.

'We're going to find him,' Ruth assured her. 'I promise you. Someone will see them. Or something will allow us to find out where Daniel is.'

As she said these words, something struck her. Something that she should have thought about earlier.

'Listen, I'm going to call you back in five minutes,' Ruth said, her mind clinging to a long shot. 'Bye.'

Nick came in with a frustrated expression. 'Bad news. The GPS tracker on James Symes' Golf hasn't been set up properly. Something to do with the SIM card. We can't use GPS to find it.'

'Bollocks.'

Nick looked at her. 'But someone is going to spot them or that Golf soon.'

'Unless she's changed vehicles,' Ruth said with an anxious expression. 'But I have thought of something.'

'Go on.'

Ruth picked up her phone. 'Daniel was going on a school trip. He told me a day or two ago that he was a bit scared about getting lost or left behind. I suggested that he download that tracking app that allows me to see where his phone is.'

'Okay,' Nick said.

'He told me that he didn't want to do that, but I've got a sneaky suspicion that he might have done it anyway and not told me. Just in case he did get lost or left behind.'

Ruth stared at her iPhone screen as she tapped the app and then tried to pair it to her number.

She held her breath. It was a long shot. After all, Daniel had told her that he wasn't going to download it.

The IOS map of North Wales appeared on her screen. *Please God, let this work.*

A green circle indicated her phone - *'Your iPhone'* - in Llancastell.

She waited for a few seconds but the map of North Wales remained clear.

Ruth felt her heart sink.

'It was worth a try,' Nick said.

Ruth gazed at the map, wondering where the hell Daniel was.

As she went to put her phone back down on her desk, she spotted something.

A green circle towards the top of the map – *Daniel's iPhone*!

'Oh my God,' she gasped, hardly daring to believe that it had actually worked. She showed the screen to Nick as he rushed over. 'He's here.'

'That's the A55, the North Wales Expressway. And that circle has just moved a fraction to the left, so they're heading west.'

'Right.' Ruth's anxiety had been replaced by focus and determination. 'Come on,' she said to Nick as she marched across the CID office and held up her iPhone. 'Right, listen up everyone. We have a hit on Daniel's mobile phone. It's on the A55 Expressway. I'm praying that he is with his phone after our wasted journey to Telford.'

'Where are they, boss?' French asked.

Ruth shook her head. In all the excitement, she'd forgotten to tell them. She looked back at the screen and saw the circle had moved from the A55. The vehicle had taken a right hand turn.

'Okay everyone,' Ruth said loudly. 'The target vehicle has just left the A55 and is now heading north on the Royal Welsh Way towards Llandudno.'

Garrow frowned. 'Why Llandudno?'

'No idea.'

'There are boats in Llandudno,' Nick pointed out. 'Maybe she's trying to get to Anglesey, but avoiding the bridges because she knows that we're looking for her.'

Ruth went over to the large map of Cheshire and North Wales. 'What else is over there?'

'Rhos on Sea,' Nick suggested.

Kennedy looked over. 'The Welsh Mountain Zoo.'

French came and looked at the map. 'The Great Orme.'

Georgie raised her head quickly as if something had registered.

'What is it, Georgie?' Ruth asked, picking up on her expression.

'The Great Orme,' Georgie said, as if this had some significance. She typed at her computer and then pointed. 'This is it. Kevin Green buried Nina Taylor's sister, Alisha, in a shallow grave on top of the Great Orme. Green claimed at his trial that the Great Orme had mythic significance to Green and his Scandinavian heritage. Apparently, it was named by Viking invaders who thought it looked like a serpent's head when they appraoched from the sea.'

'Do we think that's where Nina is going?' Ruth said. 'It has huge emotional significance for her.'

'It's the best shot we've got, boss,' Georgie said.

'Yeah, you're right,' Ruth agreed. 'Nick, how long will it take us to get there if you put your foot down?'

Nick pulled a face. 'Even flat out, the best part of an hour.'

Ruth was starting to feel overwhelmed with anxiety but she knew she had to keep it together and remain focussed. 'We haven't got an hour.' Then she had an idea. 'Get onto the NPAS and tell them I need a chopper here right now.'

The National Police Air Service – NPAS – was the section of the police force that provided helicopter support.

'I'm on it.' Nick nodded, moved swiftly away and grabbed a phone.

Ruth's heart was beating so fast that it felt as if it was out of control. She blew out her cheeks and took a deep breath, trying to compose herself.

'It's okay, boss,' Georgie reassured her. 'We're getting him back.'

'Boss,' Nick gave her the thumbs up, 'they've been monitoring the case and were on standby. Chopper will be here in ten minutes.'

Chapter 61

Ruth and Nick were standing out on an empty car park to the rear of Chester Town Hall station. She looked at her watch. It had been fifteen minutes since they'd made the call and been promised that a helicopter was on its way.

'Where the bloody hell are they?' she asked frantically. She had no idea what Nina planned to do to Daniel once they'd arrived at the Great Orme but she feared the worst.

'There they are,' Nick pointed.

The sky was just starting to lighten as the sun began to rise.

A black and yellow EC145 helicopter honed into view, circled around, and then began to descend into the middle of the car park. Its twin Turbomeca 1E2 turboshaft engines were deafening.

The wind from the rotor blades whipped around them like a tornado and Ruth had to squint. Even though it was getting light, she knew the EC145 had thermal imaging and radar on board plus enough lights to illuminate a foot-ball pitch.

'How fast does that thing go?' she shouted to Nick over the sound of the engines.

'About 160mph,' he yelled back as his jacket and shirt flapped around.

'Quicker than the Astra then,' she said with a wry expression.

'Yeah, a bit,' Nick said. 'By my calculations, we should get to the Great Orme in fifteen minutes.'

'Great,' Ruth shouted, as the doors to the helicopter opened and the crew beckoned for them to get in.

Running across the car park, they ducked under the spinning rotor blades, hopped up inside, and were immediately handed a pair of headphones to put on.

'Welcome aboard, ma'am,' the pilot said into his microphone as the doors shut and the helicopter started to lift off the tarmac immediately.

A second later, Ruth felt the helicopter pull up into the sky and her stomach pitched a little.

Please God, let us get there on time.

Chapter 62

By the time Nina had got to the car park at the summit of the Great Orme, it had started to rain. She had used another plastic tie to secure Daniel's hands, and he was sitting silently in the back. Now DI Ruth Hunter would understand the depths that she'd go to in her quest.

She parked the car and looked out at the dark inky sea that stretched out before them. The sun had started to rise, and the horizon was splashed with hues of orange and pink. However, coal-black clouds were heading their way from the east.

'It's beautiful here,' Nina said, but Daniel didn't respond. She didn't expect him to.

Glancing down at her watch, Nina saw that it was 5.10am. According to that monster Kevin Green, he had murdered her sister on the stroke of 5.30am. So it was a fitting tribute to her that the same fate should befall Daniel. A boy who would never fulfil his potential. And a boy who would never become a young man who could prey on, and destroy, women. That was the point, wasn't it? All she needed to do now was find the exact spot where Green had buried Alisha and wait.

Nina had consoled herself that this act would bring about some sense of closure for her. It evened things up in the gender war, didn't it?

'Right, we're going for a walk,' she announced in an upbeat tone.

'No,' Daniel wept. 'I don't want to go for a walk. I want you to take me home.'

'Nonsense, Daniel,' she said as she opened the driver's door. 'A walk in the fresh air will do you the world of good. I promise you.'

Getting out of the car, Nina felt the patter of fresh rain on her face. It felt refreshing and wonderful. It was as if she was being reborn today.

She opened the rear door and Daniel glared at her. 'I hate you. I'm not going anywhere with you,' he protested.

Nina leaned in and unclipped his seatbelt. 'You'll do as you're bloody told,' she sneered at him.

Daniel pushed his feet against the bottom of the driver's seat and tensed his whole body. 'I'm not getting out,' he yelled, his face now crimson. 'You can't make me!'

'Daniel, I don't want to hurt you so get out of the car!' Nina snapped.

'No!' he thundered.

Nina reached in, grabbed him by both shoulders and yanked him out of the car.

He lost his footing, and as he collapsed onto the ground his iPhone fell out of his back pocket with a clatter.

'You bloody liar!' Nina growled. 'You told me you'd had your mobile phone confiscated.'

She reached down and pulled him to his feet, his hands still tied behind his back.

'Yeah, well I didn't. And that makes you an idiot,' he said defiantly.

Nina slapped him hard across the face.

Daniel winced. His eyes were watery, but it was clear that he wasn't prepared to cry in front of her anymore.

'Right, come on,' Nina barked, looking at her watch and getting impatient. 'We're going over there,' she said, gesturing to the low, dry stone wall and the uneven grassy slope that led down to the cliff edge. It was over 700ft down from the cliff edge to the rocks and sea below.

'I told you,' Daniel said, fighting the tremor in his voice. 'I'm not going anywhere with you.'

Nina pulled out the large kitchen knife that she'd stolen from the kitchen shop in Chester and brandished it at him. 'You'll do as I say.'

Daniel swallowed hard. 'Stab me then.'

From somewhere, he'd found a new defiant resilience and Nina was getting angry.

'What?' she snarled at him.

'Just stab me. Get it over and done with,' he said, trying his best to hold it together.

Nina grabbed the top of his jacket and pulled him. He stumbled forward, but with his hands secure behind his back he was powerless to resist.

'Come on, we're running out of time,' Nina said, as she pulled him again and he stumbled forward.

'Runing out of time for what?'

'I've got someone I want you to meet,' Nina said as she forced Daniel over the low dry stone wall and onto the other side.

'What?' Daniel looked very confused. 'Who?'

'My little sister, Alisha,' Nina explained. 'She's just over here.'

Chapter 63

Looking down, Ruth could see that the helicopter was hugging the North Wales coastline as they raced west towards Llandudno and then over to the Great Orme. And what had turned out to be a spectacular summer's dawn had now been replaced by black and battleship-grey clouds as a storm moved in.

There was a rumble of thunder and then the whole sky lit up for a split second with a flash of sheet lightning.

Ruth turned to Nick who was looking lost in thought. The helicopter bumped in some turbulence and he grabbed her hand to stop her tumbling out of her seat.

'Ma'am, we should be at the target location in less than two minutes,' the pilot said over the microphone.

'Thanks,' Ruth replied as she looked at her watch. It was now 5.20pm so they had made incredibly good time over from Chester. But she felt physically sick at the thought that she might be too late.

For a moment, she saw an image of Daniel's innocent face in her mind. She remembered the moment only the day before when he'd hugged her and said that he loved living with her and Sarah. She had to bite her lip to stop the tears. What if she lost him? What would they do? It didn't bear thinking about.

They hit more turbulence and Ruth grabbed the side of the helicopter to steady herself. Rain was now starting to lash noisily against the windows and there was another deep rumble of thunder which sounded like distant gunfire.

'Ma'am, we're approaching the target location,' the pilot informed them.

Ruth had just spotted Llandudno below, and up ahead she could see the outline of the Great Orme fast approaching.

As the helicopter slowed and began to circle, Ruth gazed down at the clifftops, desperate for a sight of Daniel.

'There!' Nick said, pointing towards a car park further along.

It was James Symes' VW Golf.

Thank God their instincts had been correct that Nina was going to bring Daniel here.

With her heart thumping against the inside of her chest, Ruth looked at Nick as the helicopter began to descend towards a flat piece of grassland about fifty yards from the cliff edge.

They landed with a bump, and one of the crew immediately pulled open the door.

Ruth wasn't hanging around. She leapt from the helicopter onto the ground and ran at full pelt towards where they'd seen the Golf parked.

The noise of the helicopter's engines was deafening.

Ruth sprinted into the car park with Nick close behind.

The rain was bucketing down and her hair was already matted to her face.

'Where the hell are they?' Ruth shouted.

Nick pointed to the uneven grassy slope that led down to the cliff edge. 'They've got to be over that way somewhere,' he yelled as the rain pelted them.

There was a deafening crash of thunder that sounded as if the sky above them had split in two.

Then a blinding flash of sheet lightning that made Ruth squint as she frantically scoured the clifftops for signs of Daniel or Nina.

Out of the corner of her eye, she saw two figures traversing the path that led along the precarious edge of the Great Orme.

'Over there,' Ruth yelled, as she broke into a sprint.

Even though she'd requested authorised firearms officers to meet them there, she had no idea how long they would take. However, Nick had managed to grab an X26 Taser as they left the station.

The ground beneath her feet was hard where it had been baked dry by the summer sun.

Rain was dripping off the end of her nose as she pumped her arms.

Nina and Daniel were no longer dots in the distance, and she could see that Daniel had his hands tied behind his back.

The sight of them only made Ruth run faster.

She had no idea how she was going to rescue Daniel but she didn't care. She had to stop Nina from carrying out whatever dark plan she was about to enact at the place where her sister had been buried twenty years earlier.

Another crack of thunder above their heads. It was so loud that it made Ruth flinch.

Nina and Daniel were now only 20 yards ahead of Ruth and Nick.

As the lightning flashed again, Nina turned back to

look and immediately spotted them. She and Daniel were both drenched.

'Stop!' Ruth panted as she slowed down. There was now a sharp stabbing pain in her side from all the running.

'Ruth!' Daniel shouted as he turned and looked at her.

'Stay there!' Nina screamed as she pulled out the knife.

'Nina,' Nick said very calmy. They were now only ten yards away. 'Don't do anything stupid. Just put the knife down and we can talk.'

'No,' she snapped, her eyes wild with fury.

Ruth took another step forward, trying to give Daniel a reassuring look. 'It's okay, Daniel. It's going to be fine.' Then she looked directly at Nina. 'Let Daniel go and we can talk about this.'

Nina exploded with rage. 'I can't do that! Don't you understand? It's not time yet!'

Even though her pulse was racing, Ruth tried to give Nina an empathetic look. 'I do understand, Nina. I know what happened to you. And I know what happened to Alisha. And that's terrible and sad. And I also know about Kevin Green and his sentence which must have made you incredibly angry. But that has nothing to do with Daniel.'

'Of course it does,' Nina growled. 'It has to do with all men. Can't you see, they're all the same. Don't be so bloody naïve.' She then grabbed Daniel and, putting him in a headlock, placed the knife at his throat. 'And he's going to be just the same when he gets older. I can't allow that to happen.'

Ruth took a long calming breath. 'You can't rid the planet of the whole male gender, Nina.'

'I can do my best. And I know that others will follow me.' Nina's eyes were wide, and her breathing was fast and shallow. 'No men means no rape, no sexual assault, no paedophiles. Our streets would become a safe place overnight.'

Ruth took a step forward. 'Come on, Nina. I understand what you're saying. But Daniel has never harmed anyone, and he never will. He'll be brought up to respect women.'

Nina shook her head. 'No. Male violence towards women is instinctive. It's in their DNA.' She looked at her watch. Ruth then remembered that the newspaper article had mentioned that Green had murdered Alisha on these clifftops on the stroke of 5.30am.

To her horror, Ruth saw Nina push the blade into the skin of Daniel's neck and blood began to seep over the knife.

'NO!' she screamed.

Suddenly, Daniel smashed his head backwards so that the back of his skull cracked into Nina's nose and face.

'ARGH,' she yelled as Daniel struggled free.

She turned and slashed the knife, forcing Daniel to back away towards the cliff face.

He was only a couple of feet from the edge.

Ruth and Nick ran towards him.

Nina lunged forward with the knife again.

Daniel took a backward step, lost his footing, and then disappeared over the edge.

NOOOO!

For a moment, everything went silent.

Ruth couldn't breathe as she and Nick raced towards the edge.

Please God …

Nina blocked their path, swinging the knife in front of her.

'Get back!' she screamed.

Ruth didn't care, but the knife sliced the back of her hand and she retreated for a moment.

Daniel can't be gone …

Nick pulled out the Taser.

Nina smiled and put the knife to her own throat. 'I'm not coming with you. I'm going to meet my sister.' She sliced her throat and a torrent of blood washed over her hand.

Ruth only had thoughts for Daniel as she ran to the cliff edge and gazed down at the dark sea below.

Nothing.

Just a vast black expanse of water and razor sharp rocks hundreds of feet below.

No one could survive that fall.

Daniel was dead.

'Ruth!' cried a voice. 'Here!'

She looked down and saw someone looking up at her.

Daniel had fallen onto a rocky ledge about ten feet down the cliff face.

Thank you God!

'Stay there!' Nick shouted as he started to climb down.

'I'm scared,' Daniel said quietly.

'It's okay,' Nick reassured him. 'I'm just going to lift you up, okay?'

Daniel nodded.

Nick lifted Daniel and pushed him up.

Ruth leaned over, grabbed his shoulders and pulled him over so that he was safe.

'Thank God you're okay,' Ruth said as she wrapped her arms around him and he sobbed.

Chapter 64

Four hours later

RUTH AND SARAH were sitting at the end of Daniel's bed at home. They were elated but utterly exhausted. Daniel had been checked over by the FME – the doctor attached to a police station – who had confirmed that once his wrists had been bandaged, he could go home.

'Can I have some cereal?' he asked, sitting up in bed.

Ruth checked her watch. It was 9.30am with blazing sunshine outside, but none of them had slept a wink yet.

'Aren't you tired?' Sarah asked with a weary smile.

Daniel shook his head.

Ruth looked at him. 'But you're okay?'

He nodded, but it was clear that he was still shaken by what had happened. Ruth just hoped that there would be no long-term consequences from his ordeal.

'Crunchy nut cornflakes?' Sarah asked, getting up.

Daniel nodded and then frowned. 'You do know that my bus went nearly an hour ago.'

Ruth laughed. 'You don't have to go to school, silly. We just need you to get some sleep and rest. You've been through a lot.'

'What about tomorrow?' he asked with an excited smile.

'No,' Ruth sighed. 'You're going to need a few days off.'

'Can I play on my PlayStation?' he asked.

'Yes.' Sarah nodded. 'But I would like you to see daylight at some point. You're not a zombie.'

Daniel gave her a withering look. 'I can't be a zombie. I have to be dead and then come back to life to be a zombie.'

For a moment, Ruth got a flash of the moment Daniel fell from the cliff top at the Great Orme. It still made her stomach lurch.

'Can we have a Chinese takeaway tonight?' he asked with an impish look in his eyes.

Ruth laughed. 'Hey, you're pushing your luck now buster.'

'Ignore grumpy here,' Sarah joked. 'You can have anything you want.'

Ruth looked at her and raised her eyebrow. 'You might come to regret that comment.'

Chapter 65

48 hours later

RUTH WAS STANDING for the last time in front of the CID team at Chester Town Hall nick. She could see that although they were exhausted, they were also pleased that they'd finally got a result of sorts. Coppers were always frustrated when they weren't able to bring a criminal to trial so that the victims and their families could get justice. Doing that allowed them some feeling of closure. Nina taking her own life had robbed them of that.

'Morning everyone,' Ruth said with a coffee in her hand as she perched on a table. The scene boards – covered in photos, maps, documents and writing – were still up. They would be until after the internal inquiry. 'As you know, we're leaving you today, so I want to thank you for all your incredible work on this case. You really did go above and beyond. And you should be proud of yourselves.'

Kennedy looked over. 'I think I speak for everyone here when I say that it's been impressive the way you've stepped up as SIO. And it's been a pleasure to be on your team, boss.'

'After a bit of a shaky start?' Ruth joked.

Kennedy smiled and gave a little shrug. 'Yeah, it was a bit of a shaky start.'

There was laughter from some of the team.

'A cockney woman from North Wales,' Ruth quipped. 'I bet you wondered what you'd let yourselves in for.'

More laughter.

'Right, there is some boring stuff to go through I'm afraid,' Ruth explained.

There were some jokey groans, especially from Nick. She gave him a good-humoured look.

'Obviously we've called in the IOPC,' Ruth said.

Formerly the Independent Police Complaints Commission (IPCC), the Independent Office for Police Conduct was formed in 2018 and was the body responsible for complaints and allegations of police misconduct. In a case as complicated and serious as Nina Taylor, the IOPC would scrutinise that every part of the investigation was handled correctly. Ruth was anxious about what the IOPC would make of Nina Taylor's escape from Chester Crown Court. Ruth would be interviewed about the incident some time in the future and she might even face disciplinary proceedings if she or Nick were found to be negligent in Nina's escape. After all, James Symes was murdered by her while she was on the run.

'My suggestion is that you go through everything with a fine tooth comb,' Ruth said. 'You know what they're like. Every witness statement typed up, evidence requests signed off on. You know the drill but I don't want anyone in here to get caught out.' Ruth cast her eyes around the room and gave a tentative smile. 'You will be seeing me again when the IOPC inspectors come calling. But until then, thanks again.'

As she moved away from the front of the CID office, the Chester CID team gave her a round of applause. She couldn't help but give a modest smile. She didn't think she deserved it.

Ruth arrived at the seats where the Llancastell team were sitting.

Nick gave her a wry smile. 'Hey, you're a hit.'

'Yeah, and you lot never give me a round of applause,' she joked. Then she pointed towards the doors. 'We'd better head back across the border.'

As they made their way across the office, Ruth spotted Kennedy sitting at her computer.

Ruth went over to her. 'I didn't want to single you out in front of everyone but you've been a great help.'

'Thanks,' Kennedy said, but she looked perturbed. 'Unfortunately, DI Weaver is coming back next week, rumour has it.'

Ruth raised an eyebrow. 'You don't get on?'

'Between you and me, he's a complete mysogynist,' Kennedy said under her breath. 'I'm looking to transfer out of here.'

Ruth thought for a second. 'Ever thought about North Wales?'

Kennedy's face brightened. 'Are you being serious?'

'Yes,' Ruth replied. 'You're an excellent copper and we have the budget for a DS. What do you think?'

'I think yes,' Kennedy laughed.

'Put in your transfer papers,' Ruth said, 'and we'll make it happen.'

Kennedy had a beaming smile. 'Thank you.'

'I'll be seeing you soon then, Jade,' Ruth said, returning her smile as she headed back towards the exit.

They were about to get a new member of the Llancastell CID team and she was just what they needed.

Chapter 66

Georgie stretched out on the sofa and sipped at her mug of tea. She thought that she'd really miss having a glass of wine or beer in the evenings, but she didn't at all.

Glancing out through the window, she saw that it was getting dark. She got up and went over to the curtains, still slightly apprehensive about the mystery stalker. But she told herself that she was an experienced copper who could handle herself.

The cul-de-sac outside was deserted and a couple of the streetlights had just come on, throwing a lovely warm vanilla light across the road and gardens.

As she began to close the curtains she saw something out of the corner of her eye. Someone was moving very slowly towards her front door.

Instead of feeling frightened, Georgie was now angry. How dare someone think it's okay to prowl around her house at night, scaring her.

Even though she knew it was completely reckless, she marched into the kitchen, grabbed the biggest kitchen knife she could find and moved swiftly towards the door.

Putting her eye to the spyhole, she saw that a figure was standing on her doorstep.

Right, I've had enough of this!

Swinging open the front door, Georgie brandished the knife and yelled, 'Right, who the fuck are you and what the hell do you want?'

Her voice echoed around the whole close.

The hooded figure on the doorstep was holding another simple bunch of flowers.

He looked terrified and his eyes widened in fear.

And it was then that Georgie realised that he was a kid.

He couldn't have been more than 14-years-old!

What the …?

'Right, get in here,' she barked at him.

'I'm sorry but …' the boy muttered nervously.

Georgie gestured to her hallway. 'Get in here. I want a word with you right now.'

The boy took a step forward, handed her the flowers apologetically and then went inside.

'In here,' Georgie snapped at him, gesturing to the door to the living room.

'I'm really sorry,' the boy said, sounding like he was about to cry.

They went in and Georgie pointed to the sofa. 'Sit down there. And for God's sake, put that bloody hood down.'

'Sorry,' he said, as he pulled his hoodie down and sat huddled on the sofa blinking nervously.

'What's your name?' Georgie said, sounding a little calmer.

'Luke,' he murmured. 'Please don't tell my mum.'

'What the hell are you playing at Luke?' she asked, shaking her head. 'You've been scaring me to death.'

'I'm really sorry, I …' Luke was lost for words.

Georgie looked directly at him. 'What's with the flowers?'

He looked very embarrassed and shrugged.

'Look, I'm going out on a limb here,' Georgie said, 'but do you have a crush on me? Is that why you were out the back and why you've brought me flowers?'

He paused and then nodded.

'But I'm old enough to be your mother, Luke,' Georgie groaned as she shook her head. Then she patted her tummy. 'And I'm pregnant.'

There were a few seconds of silence.

'I'm going to need you to promise me something,' she said.

Luke nodded, but he looked like he wanted the ground to open up and swallow him.

'Never *ever* go into someone's garden again. And don't peer into anyone's window at night, okay?' she said in a serious tone.

Luke nodded again.

'I need to hear you say it, Luke.'

'I promise …' he muttered.

'Because people will think you're a pervert and a weirdo if you do that,' Georgie explained. 'And if you get caught by the wrong person snooping around their house, you might get very badly hurt. Do you understand?'

'Yes. Sorry.'

'And I think you need to find a girl who is roughly the same age as you. And if you think she's attractive, just talk to her. However scary that might be. Be kind and respectful. Make her laugh,' Georgie said. 'And don't do anything like this ever again.'

Luke glanced at her apologetically. 'I won't. I promise.'

Chapter 67

3 days later

AS RUTH PARKED her car on her driveway, she let out an audible sigh. It was only 6pm and it was going to be a beautiful summer's evening. She had stopped to get wine and food for a barbeque – she couldn't wait. As she got out, she noticed a car that she didn't recognise outside.

We're not expecting anyone are we? she wondered.

She put her key into the front door and opened it.

Silence.

'Hello?' she called out loudly.

Nothing.

Someone came out of the living room.

It startled her.

It was Sarah. She had a strange expression on her face.

'Everything all right?' Ruth asked, starting to feel uneasy.

Sarah gestured to the living room. 'Our social worker

Susannah is here,' she said quietly. 'She's in there with Daniel.'

'Okay,' Ruth said cautiously.

'We're just discussing our adoption application,' Sarah explained. 'Do you want to come and join us?'

Ruth couldn't tell from Sarah's tone or expression if it was good or bad news about Daniel's adoption.

She followed Sarah down the hallway and into the living room.

Enjoy this book?
Get the next book in the series
'The Llangollen Killings'
My Book - link to Amazon UK
https://www.amazon.com/dp/B0CXF1KZBG

The Llangollen Killings
A Ruth Hunter Crime Thriller #Book 19

Your FREE book is waiting for you now

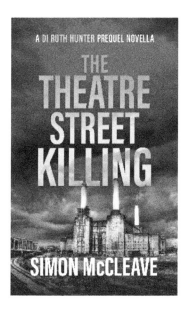

Get your FREE copy of the prequel to
the DI Ruth Hunter Series NOW
http://www.simonmccleave.com/vip-email-club
and join my VIP Email Club

DC RUTH HUNTER SERIES

London, 1997. A series of baffling murders. A web of political corruption. DC Ruth Hunter thinks she has the brutal killer in her sights, but there's one problem. He's a Serbian war criminal who died five years earlier and lies buried in Bosnia.

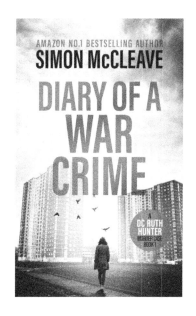

My Book
My Book

AUTHOR'S NOTE

Although this book is very much a work of fiction, it is located in Snowdonia, a spectacular area of North Wales. It is steeped in history and folklore that spans over two thousand years. It is worth mentioning that Llancastell is a fictional town on the eastern edges of Snowdonia. I have made liberal use of artistic licence, names and places have been changed to enhance the pace and substance of the story.

Acknowledgments

I will always be indebted to the people who have made this novel possible.

My mum, Pam, and my stronger half, Nicola, whose initial reaction, ideas and notes on my work I trust implicitly. Carole Kendal for her meticulous proofreading. My designer Stuart Bache for yet another incredible cover design. My superb agent, Millie Hoskins at United Agents, and Dave Gaughran for his invaluable support and advice. And Keira Bowie for her ongoing patience and help.

Made in the USA
Las Vegas, NV
08 April 2024

88425249R00164